WESLEY

BISHOP'S SNOWY LEAP BOOK 3

KATHI S. BARTON

World Castle Publishing, LLC
Pensacola, Florida
Copyright © Kathi S. Barton 2020
Paperback ISBN: 9781953271181
eBook ISBN: 9781953271198
First Edition World Castle Publishing, LLC, September 21, 2020
http://www.worldcastlepublishing.com
Licensing Notes
Cover: Karen Fuller
Editor: Maxine Bringerberg

Chapter 1

The equipment was larger than life. It didn't so much scare her, but it did intimidate her something terrible. Emmie waited at the end of the row that Wesley was putting in for pea planting. He'd told her just this morning he'd never realized what real anticipation was until he had to wait months and months for something so simple as peas. Waving at him when he looked in her direction, she wondered how hard it would be to run over one of her brothers with the sucker.

"You all right?" She nodded at him and thanked him again for allowing her to hide out in his house while her brothers were around. "It's not a problem. You keep cooking for me like you are, and I might just keep you around."

"You'd not like having me beaten up all the time if any one of my brothers shows up. You're a good man, Wesley."

He was embarrassed, and she had to laugh. "I've been called into the bank for a little bit. While I know Dutch is in jail, I'm still afraid to head into town. I don't suppose you can call one of your brothers to take me in, can you?"

"I can do you one better. Raven, I think you know her?" She said she knew of her. "She's scarier than your brothers. Smarter too. But then that's not all that hard. Anyway, she's on her way here to get some information on the tractors I've been using for her grandma. I know you might not be too thrilled to have your brothers arrested, but they've been—"

"If anyone can get them off the streets and out of my life, I'm all for it. Penny and her grandda are going to meet me at the bank. They have some clothing for me from Mr. Joe's house." He said that was good. "You've been a real hero for me, Wesley. I don't think anyone else would have just taken in a stranger like you did. I can't thank you enough."

"It wasn't anything. As I told you this morning, you've been really nice having around. Stems off some of the loneliness I didn't realize I was having." When he got down off the tractor, Emmie was again surprised by his height. She wasn't a little person at five-eleven, but he seemed to tower over her. "Am I making you uncomfortable?"

"At first, you did. But for whatever reason, I feel safe around you. Since we both know we're not mates or whatever white tigers call their other half, I'm assuming you're just a nice guy." He threw back his head and laughed, and Emmie couldn't help it, she joined him. "I've only been here for three days, and I don't think I've had this much fun in all my life."

"The same with me. All right. I'm finished helping the neighbors with their fields, and I have about an hour before I have to meet my dad and his cronies over at Mom's again with the tractor, so how about I just run you in? You've been great for helping me get my stuff packed up to move, so I'm going to treat you to something you don't have to cook." She thought she could fix something the house, but being waited on sounded too good to pass up. "I just need to take a quick shower and change. Even with air in that sucker, it still gets mighty hot when I'm working."

He did take a quick shower and was ready to go in less than twenty minutes. By the time they'd pulled into the bank parking lot, she was just nervous enough that she felt slightly ill. Wesley didn't say anything to her or even tease her as she sat there. When she told him she was ready, he still hadn't made fun of her, nor had he hit her. Emmie thought she could get used to this.

Mr. Joe was sitting on one of the many benches in the bank. After he shook hands with Wesley and thanked him, Mr. Joe hugged her like he'd not seen her in years. Letting him hold her while he seemed to gather himself, she took him into her office so they could wait for Penny to return from the store across the street, Mr. Joe told her.

"I think being thirsty all the time is making me a little nervous. Penny too. She's taking me by the doc's office after we leave here. I'm not even gonna argue with her about it. I think she gets enough of that from our stupid family." Mr. Joe was sitting in one of the most comfortable chairs in her office, which wasn't really saying much. They were all about as comfortable as sitting on a slab of concrete. "You'd think for as much business as you're bringing into this little bank, they'd be happy to spring for new chairs. This one is worse than my old mattress at home."

Penny entered the room and kissed them both. She sat down beside Mr. Joe. While she didn't have any idea what they were going to need, Emmie closed her office door and locked it, a habit she'd gotten into when she lived at home. Locking her door always afforded her just enough time to know someone was about to enter her room.

"You doing all right out there with Wesley, child?" She told him she was doing great. He was a wonderful man. "He is at that. All them Bishop boys are as good as gold. Their parents, they did a great job of passing down their kindness to them. I'm here to fix some things that I've been meaning to do for some time now. First and foremost, honey, I'd like for you to make sure the account Wendy had is closed up from her kids."

"It is. As soon as I heard about her death, I locked hers and your accounts. I hope I didn't cause you any trouble with that." He said he'd not noticed. "Good. I figured you'd have your hands full with the other two around, and I didn't want them coming in and trying to cash out your account. Also, I did put a reminder out to the people who work here that your account could be touched by you and only you, Penny. I figured that would save you a great deal of heartache as well."

"Thank you so much. I would never have thought of that." Emmie told her she'd do the same for her if they were in the same situation. "I owe you so much, Emmie. Had you not talked to me about your brothers, I might well have been six feet under by now. They're already pissed because I'm not allowing them to sponge off Grandpa Joe. The police have been really good about having someone watch his house. They had to run in my dad and his brother earlier today. They were in Grandma's house, moving their crap in. She's not even in the ground, and they're already shoving her things to the side of the road."

After they were finished with all the changes Mr. Joe wanted, they set up a reading of the will with an attorney. A friend of the family, Mr. Brooks Hall, wasn't the attorney that had handled Wendy's will in the first place, but he said he'd be happy to come to them anytime to read the will. Apparently, everyone mentioned in the will was right there in the room. Her sons weren't even named in it.

"That's going to cause a fuss, I think. Well, it'll be more than a fuss, but you understand." Mr. Joe laughed and said he'd been the one to write out what the will was to say, and since Wendy couldn't read all that well, she was more than happy to have him take care of things.

"I figured what little money she had should go to the one that helped her the most. Them boys of hers, they were jerks all their life to their mother. And it's doubtful to me that her brother or sister will come around. They didn't have too much to do with her after she moved into that house. Not that she ever noticed it." Grandpa shook his head. "I'm telling you right now that my will is simple. What I have goes to the two of you."

"I'm not really your granddaughter, Mr. Joe. I mean, I love that you think of me that way, but all I've ever been is a very close friend to Penny." Mr. Joe said that was good enough for him. "Thank you so much. I don't know what to say. Only that you'd better not be thinking of leaving us anytime soon. I need you as much as your flesh and blood does."

"And I need you two girls around too. Why, just the other day, I was thinking that a parent shouldn't have to outlive a child. But then I got to thinking about how much drama I was going to be out of. I loved my Wendy—more than I should have, I think—but she gave me you, Penny, then, in turn, Emmie here. A great-granddaughter and a little girl that I've loved more than anything."

Emmie was just finishing up when one of the tellers knocked and was let in. She looked upset, and it took her five minutes to let her know that James Harold was in the bank demanding to have his mother's money.

"He threatened me with harm, Miss Emmie. I mean, he said that not only would he ruin my body so not even dental records would be helpful in identifying me, but that he'd kill my entire family. I can't work that way." Emmie told her to have a seat, and she'd take care of him. "You should know I've buzzed the police too. I never would have thought we'd use those security buttons until today."

The police plus Sawyer came in just as she was headed to the slot Shelly had been at. She asked James what she could do for him. After a short round of cursing, he finally told her what he'd been trying to do.

"I want all my mom's money in my hand right now." She told him no and asked if he needed anything else. "What the hell do you mean, no? It's not your money, it's mine now that she's dead. Give it over, Emmie, or so help me, I'm going to kill you. I need it."

"I'm sure you do since you've not had a job in— I was going to say in a long time, but I don't think I've never known you to have one. But you're not getting anything from the account because the will hasn't been read." James told her to fuck the will. "While that is tempting, I don't think it's physically possible. Now, you go about your day and try very hard not to piss anyone else off, or so help me, James, I will have these nice men behind you keep you in the cell right beside Dutch. You're not going to get into her account."

He turned when Sawyer laughed and asked him what the fuck he was doing there. James told him he thought he'd been fired. "Nah. I'm still a cop. I help the police out when they ask, especially when they have to go collect an idiot from the banks. You should really leave here now, James. Because if she has to tell you again, you're not getting the money, I'm going to have one of these fine officers blow your head off."

It was then Emmie noticed that every other customer in the bank was leaving. This might not end well, and the home office was going to be pissy about it, but she didn't want anyone harmed by James. Or anyone for that matter. Sawyer put his hand on James's shoulder, and it was over before James was able to pull the trigger on his gun.

While James lay screaming on the floor about his right to the money, with the other man's boot at his neck, Sawyer asked her if she was all right. Emmie didn't think she'd been all right in a long time, but told him she was fine. Then he asked her if she wanted to press charges.

"I do, as does Shelly Crabapple, one of the tellers that works here. She told me he threatened her as well. I know you're more than likely aware of it, but James here isn't supposed to have a weapon. He's been convicted of a crime, and only just got out of prison a month ago." Sawyer told her he'd not known but thanked her. "Anytime. Wesley is outside. Would you mind asking him if he'd escort us home? I have Penny as well as Mr. Joe in my office right now."

"Good idea. Wesley might look all relaxed like he'd not hurt a fly, but we all know better." She thanked him. "It's fine, Emmie. Also, Raven, my wife, she might come by the house later to talk to you about some of the other things she has on her list from yours and Penny's family."

"I don't know where we're going to be after today. I

don't want to wear out my welcome with Wesley. You should also know, my brothers are on the same warpath as this one is. I've been staying at Wesley's home for a couple of days now." He said he knew that. "I figured as much. Thanks for keeping an eye on them for us."

"Mr. Joe is a good friend to our family. And by extension, you are as well." Again, she thanked him. Wesley came in and told her he was going to lock up and sit out there to wait for her to be finished. For her to take her time. "I'm going to keep an eye out for those brothers of yours too, Emmie. They'll regret any kind of move they make to hurt any of you."

James was still under Sawyer's foot, and his threats were becoming more violent and creative. Emmie had to think that when he was let go, he'd be up and trying something stupid with Sawyer. As soon as she thought that, one of the officers with Sawyer cuffed James by his wrists.

"You're fucking going to pay for this, bitch." She pointed out she'd done nothing more than tell him no. "You think that's all? Well, I got news for you. You're not going to be telling me no again."

"That doesn't even make sense." He lunged at her, and she was glad she didn't even flinch when he did it. "Get out of here, James, before I think of another thing to bring up about you. Stupidity, sadly, isn't cause for an arrest, or you'd have been jailed a long time before now."

Wesley joined her in the office as soon as she locked

down the bank. The police would take the footage of today, and she'd send a copy of it to the home office. Today was turning out better than she could have planned it to be.

~*~

Wesley tried his best not to stare at the other woman. He knew he was making her uncomfortable, but he just couldn't believe she was the granddaughter of Wendy Harold. Not only that, but her uncle was one of the worst kinds of people in the world. Tony wasn't too bad, not really, but he was an odd noodle at times.

"Are you going to take a picture or something?" Wesley just smiled at her when Mr. Joe laughed. "The way you're eyeing me, I feel like I have something in my hair. I know for a fact I don't."

"You don't. I'm sorry for staring, but I was just thinking about your relatives. I can't believe you are part of the same gene pool." Her face told him she didn't believe a word he'd just said to her. "Honestly. First, there is Wendy. I've known her all my life. You? I didn't even know Tony was married, much less had a daughter that looks like a goddess. I'm assuming you look like your mother. You certainly don't look like your dad."

"You look just like your father. You could almost be his twin." He thanked her. "I don't know who my mother is. I never knew, as a matter of fact. So I think you might be right on that. I'm sorry for giving you a hard time. Things just haven't been going right for the last few days. Well, that's not true. Not going right for most of my life."

"I know your uncle and dad as well. You and Emmie are the opposite of your family in just about any way you wish to compare yourself to them." She thanked him this time. "No worries. I was coming into town anyway. Emmie and I are having lunch together."

He could tell she was disappointed, but when Emmie invited her friend and Mr. Joe to come with them, he was glad for it. It would be fun to get to know this woman a lot better. He picked up the book he'd gotten at the library earlier today and started reading it.

Wesley realized he'd read the same page six times or more while he was waiting on the group to be finished up. It wasn't normal for him to do that, not be able to tune things out around him while he read. But today, with this group and especially Penny, he just couldn't concentrate.

He stood up when they said they were finished, and they headed to the pizza shop across the street. Going to the door first, he held it open for the other three, who went in ahead of him. Penny's scent nearly took him to his knees. Standing in the doorway so that his mind could catch up with what his nose just told him, it was Mr. Joe that came to get him.

"Are you all right, son?" He nodded at him, and couldn't have stopped the smile on his face with a gun to his head. "Son, you're scaring this old man. What's wrong? You can tell me anything, and I'd not say a word to anyone."

"Penny is your great-granddaughter." It wasn't a

question, but he nodded anyway. "She's my mate, Mr. Joe. I didn't expect to find her at all, much less in a pizza joint."

Mr. Joe laughed. "Well, I guess this is about the best news I've heard in a while. Congratulations. But I think you should close the door there. People are beginning to wonder if you have all your marbles. It's chilly out." Wesley laughed and let the door swing shut. "You going to tell her? I'd like to be right there when you do. I don't rightly know how she'll take it, but you have to tell her. She'll be safer with you than anywhere else she can hide out."

They both sat down, and he picked up the menu to think. He was never so glad to have a big house to go to than he was right now. Putting the menu in the middle of the table when the waitstaff came to take their order, he looked at Mr. Joe first.

"Raven purchased all of us brothers of Sawyer a home. Mom and Dad are having one built that they're excited about. I'm moving into mine tomorrow. It's been repainted, as well as the carpets cleaned. There are about ten bedrooms in the place." Mr. Joe told him he was lucky to have such a generous person in his family. "Yes, I think so too. I was wondering if the three of you would like to come and live there with me. It'll have plenty of room for us all. Not to mention, it has an indoor pool I'm excited about playing around in. My mate will be there too, so it wouldn't be anything but family around."

"That's a very nice thing, both the house and inviting

us to stay. However, I can't imagine your mate would be all that keen on you having an elderly man and two single women in your home." He told Penny that only one of them was single. "I don't understand. You said your mate will be there too."

"She will be. If she wishes. I just think you guys will be safer in a big house that your other family doesn't know about than the ones you live in now." Penny looked at Emmie, then back at him. Then she asked him if Emmie was his mate. "No."

It took her several seconds to figure out what he was saying. She stood up and sat down a total of three times before she glared at him. He thought her adorable when she told him he wasn't funny but wisely kept that to himself.

"You could have just said that when we were at the bank." He said he'd not figured it out until they came in here. "Why the roundabout way of telling me? Is this your way of doing everything? I will tell you right now, I don't think you're the least bit funny."

"You'd not be the first person to tell me that. However, I was working up to telling you. I didn't want to just blurt it out and have you toss your salad in my face." Penny glared harder. "You really should stop that now, Penny. You're even more beautiful when you're pissed at me. Not that I don't blame you, but you are my mate, and the offer of you three staying with me stands. Things are going to get nastier as the next few days go by."

"I, for one, would love to live with you, Wesley." He thanked Mr. Joe without taking his eyes off Penny. "Those boys of Wendy's aren't going to take too kindly to the reading of the will. Scratch that. I think the only one that will care is James. And you know as well as I do, Penny, that when James is pissed off, so are the Donnelly boys. They feed off each other."

"I don't want to. I will, but I really don't want to." Wesley nodded at Penny. "I mean, I really don't want to live with you, but I'm thinking you're right. We'd all be safer in a house rather than an apartment, or even Grandpa Joe's home. It's not very big either, and we'd be falling all over each other in no time. I'll live there, but I'm not going to sleep with you."

"All right. I can understand that. We barely know one another, and I won't take advantage of you. I have some furniture in the house. Holly, Raven's grandma, sold her house to my brother, and she had a great many things still in storage. After Chandler got what he wanted, the rest of us took what was left. I gladly took the other bedroom suites to be in my home. The others, my brothers, took the things for the living room, feeling they'd be in there more than they would in any of the other rooms." Their subs were brought to the table, and he dug into his as he continued. "I have a live-in cook as well. Her name is Caroline. She's a member of my brother Sawyer's leap and needed to have a place she could call her own. Her family was all gone, moving away to have better paying jobs. I was lucky enough to have a place for her to live in on the property."

Wesley answered all the questions put to him. Most of them were from Mr. Joe, about his planting in the spring, as well as his helping the others around town. He told them about the tractor and the attachments he had been trying out and loved.

"They just gave you a tractor worth more than a house for nothing?" He told Penny what had happened that he ended up owning it. "Okay, I guess I can see a company doing that. Having a farmer that no one knows trying it out and then telling others would make for good cover. Congratulations on that. I have to admit, I do miss having fresh vegetables all the time. Grandma always had fresh food from her little garden. What she didn't eat, she'd put up. Do people still do that?"

"My mom does. Jellies and jams mostly. Here in the last couple of years, she's been donating what she can't put up to different people around the town. You'd be surprised how far a couple of rows of green beans can go when you're as good as we are about taking care of our gardens." He realized then that just the other day, he'd been bitching about having a mate to his brothers and him only being a lowly farmer. However, right now, he thought he had the best job of all. His mate was into fresh things as much as he was. "Today I was going to put the tractor and the implements away until early spring. I was even able to put in a garden for my mom this year, and decided to grow some fresh peas in the early spring."

They talked all through their meal. When they brought the check, he was more than happy to pick it up and pay. He noticed that all three of his lunch guests put down money for a tip. Being glad they'd not put too little on the table, he still added more to the bill when he paid.

"Where is your home? I have a feeling it's close to your parents' place." He told Penny it was, but it also had a large barn and a place for him to play around in. "I'm not sleeping with you, Wesley. I'm not easy, and I won't put out just because you're keeping my family safe."

"I wouldn't have it any other way, Penny." She cocked a brow at him. "I'm serious. I don't know you anymore than you do me. I'd like to take our time, get to know each other before we go right to the making love part." She said she might not ever want to have sex with him. "So long as you're happy, then I will be too."

She snorted at him when she walked away. They walked to the new home, his first time seeing it in the daylight, and he was glad now that he carried around the keys to the place. Wesley handed the second set to Penny, so she could come and go when she wanted while here, he told her. Wesley was thrilled when she didn't toss them back in his face.

The house looked beautiful with the new walls and the hardwood floors all shiny from their treatment. Every room they explored, he was just as pleased with it as they seemed to be. The kitchen, where Ms. Caroline was making a list, had been updated recently, and a pantry had been put in. Penny seemed to be more impressed with the kitchen area than she had been about the indoor pool.

"I love to bake. Would that be a problem for you, Ms. Caroline?" When the older woman looked at him, Penny answered her unspoken concern. "He claims I'm his mate and that we'll be living here with him. No hanky panky, but we'll be safer here, I think."

"If Wesley says you're his mate, then you can count on it being true. You couldn't find you a better family to be getting into either." Penny thanked her. "Now then. Yes, you come on in here and bake all you want, mistress. I've never been known to bake all that much, but I'd surely like to have the smells coming from here. You just give me a list of what you need, and I'll order it with the rest of the kitchen stock-up."

While they worked on the list, he moved into the living room and looked around. There was a great deal of open space in this area, and he hadn't a clue how to fill it. While he didn't watch all that much television, he would like to have a nice sized one for this room. He thought it might be necessary for the sheer size of the room so you could see it.

"I don't have to move in here with you, Wesley." He turned to look at Emmie and asked her why not. "Well, you have a new mate, for which I'm so happy for you both, and Grandpa Joe living here. I'm not related to either of them, as you know. Also, I have been hiding out on my own for a very long time."

"There isn't a single reason I can think of that would make me want to have you not move in here with us. And you are family. I know Mr. Joe thinks of you as his great-granddaughter as much as he does Penny." He smiled at her then. "You know my parents. If they found out I was shoving you out to live someplace in the woods as you wanted that first day, Mom would take me to the woodshed in a minute and make me change my mind about being too old for that particular punishment."

"I don't want to be a bother to any of you." He assured her she wouldn't be. "All right then. You will tell me if I've overstayed my welcome. Right?"

"I promise you, Emmie, I don't have a doubt in the world that you're going to be as much a part of my family as you are to Mr. Joe and Penny. Besides, I think with you here, Penny will feel more comfortable. And believe it or not, I want her happy no matter what." She mentioned her brothers. "Don't you worry about any of them. I'm going to have the police, as well as my family, making sure you're all safe and sound. I just ask that when you do go out, don't do it alone. Nor to go out without telling us where you're going and when you'll be back. I don't want to have to worry that they might have hurt you when you're in my care."

"You're a good man, Wesley. And a good friend. I hope you can make sure they're not going to harm any of us. I have a feeling they won't just hurt us the next time but will try and kill us. Especially Grandpa Joe." He asked her why. "Because Grandpa Joe is a very wealthy man. More so than anyone in this world gives him credit for."

"I'll keep that in mind when we're out." He hugged her back when she hugged him. "Thank you, Emmie. Without you being the bank manager, it might have been years before I met Penny. I owe you a great deal."

"Pay me back by making sure she's safe. And happy. I know you will, so I'm not worried about it, but I don't want her to be hurt or sad." He said he could do that. "See that you do. I love both those people more than I do anyone else."

Chapter 2

Dutch looked around for his sister. She was supposed to meet him at noon. It was now two minutes till the hour, and she wasn't there. If a person showed up on the dot, or even five minutes till the time they'd agreed on, he would consider them late. He despised people who showed up on time or late. And she damned well knew it.

"I'm here." She sat down across from him and smiled. "Whatever it is, Dutch, I'm not buying into it. In the event you don't know what that means, I'm not bailing you out. I sort of like you being here. I'm not going to find you an attorney and pay for it. Or, for that matter, I'm not going to do anything for you. You're on your own."

"Are you finished spouting off shit you think I'm going to want you to do?" She smiled at him, and had he not been cuffed up like an animal, he'd have hit her square in the mouth. "You will do what I tell you on all that shit,

Emmie. You *will* bail me out. Today, as a matter of fact. You *are* going to find me an attorney. A good one too. Not those pieces of shit that the state turns over for people to use. And you *will* do whatever I tell you, or you'll face me."

"Technically, I'm facing you now." Another grin and his anger was nearly making him blind with the need to hit her. "But besides me not helping you out, I'm going to press more charges against you simply because—and you might not believe this—I'm getting a backbone where you're concerned. You and Butch have hurt me for far too long, and I'm putting my foot down. No more, Dutch."

He tried lunging at her, and all he did was scoot the table more in her direction. It also pulled his shoulders since he'd been hog-tied to the stupid thing since before she'd gotten there. He didn't even make any sort of impression on her when he growled. That usually had her cowering in the corner someplace. This time, all she did was laugh at him. Christ, he hated his sister.

"If there isn't anything else, Dutch, I'm going home. I have so much to do today." He told her she wasn't going anywhere and to sit her ass down. "No. I'm not your whipping girl anymore, and I do what I want. It's freeing to have someone in my corner. I never had you there. You should have been, you being my brother and all. Also, if by chance you ever get out of here—upright, that is—I will move away to where you'll never be able to find me."

"You go on thinking that, bitch, and that'll be the day."

She asked him what the hell he was saying. He didn't know either but wasn't going to allow her to make fun of him. "You know exactly what I mean. You try and hide from me, and I'll find you without any trouble."

"Yes, well, whatever. You barely have enough chain to squat, so you being able to hurt me isn't even a scary thought in my head." She moved away from him and then came back. Laying a small white envelope on the table, she laughed. "That is for you to do with as you wish. It's the phone number of the county seat. They'll be able to find you an attorney much faster than you can. As I said, don't call me again, Dutch. Nor do I want you to have the people here do it. I'm finished with you."

He continued to scream for her to get back there as he was being taken back to his cell. Fucking cunt was going to get it, just as soon as he could get out of there. However, he wasn't so sure that was going to be as easy as he'd hoped. The cop that had picked him up at his grandpa's house yesterday said he had seven outstanding warrants for him, as well as having a gun on him when he was arrested. That was a violation of his parole, and they didn't take too kindly to that.

Dutch was what they called a three striker. No matter how small the crime this time, he was headed back to the big house. And he'd not be getting out for good behavior. Not that he had ever had that happen to him, but it had been nice to dream about it.

Once he was back in his tiny cell, he thought hard on

how he was going to get out of there. There were plenty of options, one of them being just what Emmie had said—in a body bag. Or not upright, she'd told him. He wasn't too keen on that one, so he moved to the second option.

This one was riskier. It involved him getting a gun and shooting his way out. That would have him ending up on the shit end of cops coming after him. Cops didn't care for you shooting their own kind. They had this kind of pact, he thought, where all the cops around the world would kill your ass simply because you had the nerve to kill a cop. Because as surely as he was sitting there, the only way he could think to get them off his back was to die himself. Again, he didn't want that to happen.

Dutch could escape, he supposed, but he wasn't sure how that was going to fly either. This place might give the illusion of being a shitty jail, but they had the most advanced equipment he'd ever seen. Even the locks on the cell doors were complicated. Not only were there locks on them that used a key, but there were electrical things that he didn't understand how to work.

When his tray of food was brought to him, he watched as it was scanned for a bar code on the top, then the one he assumed that was on his cell. After that, it was pushed under the bars. There was always a second person with the food cart. He or she would hold a gun on him until the cart was moved to the next cell, like they were terrified that he might shove the tray back to them or something. Whatever their reasons, they weren't taking any chances with him getting the wrong food or getting out altogether.

Dutch began eating his food, which really wasn't all that bad. It was better than he'd gotten while in the bigger prison. He'd been able to pick out his lunch from the three that were being offered—the same with breakfast and dinner. He glanced over at the privacy curtain, they'd called it, that was near his toilet. Even though it was clear, he closed it every time he had to use it.

He knew James was there too. They'd spoken a couple of times since he'd been brought in. James had a to do at the bank and hadn't been able to get his mom's money out of the bank. Which wasn't right either. Dutch just knew that his sister had something to do with James being arrested. He'd not put it past her to have something to do with him being there too.

When one of the cops came down the hall, he wondered what was going on. He knew James had been fucking pissed at Emmie, but surely they couldn't add shit onto him on account of her—could they? Emmie should have been smothered in her crib a long time ago, Dutch thought. But the cop stopped in front of James's cage.

"You got yourself a visitor, James. You want them to come back here or want me to tell him to go away? Up to you. If I have to take you to him, you're going to be jacked up like you were before." James told the man that was a shitty thing to do. "If you say so. I don't have time to go behind you and wipe your ass, either. Tell him to come or go? It's up to you."

"Tell them to come back then." James cursed the man under his breath. "Mother fucker. He probably could have told him what he wanted, and that would have been the end of it. Now I have to sit here and listen to some fuck and be bored out of my mind."

"Emmie was in earlier. She was spouting off shit that she claims she'd not going to be doing for me. I set her ass straight on that." James told him how she'd been in the bank earlier and had been the one to tell him he wasn't getting any money. "It's your momma's money, right? How can she do that? You don't have to worry about that, James. I'll take care of her when I get out of here."

~*~

The man sat down across from James. He was well dressed, his suit looking like it cost more than Dutch had made on his last heist. As soon as he pulled out a small notebook, James asked him what the fuck he was there for. He told him his name before he started speaking about why he was there.

"I was sent here to tell you the gist of the will of Wendy Harold. I want you to know that while you weren't mentioned in the will at all, your sister wanted to make sure you understood that—"

"Hold on there. What do you mean, I wasn't mentioned in the will? I'm her son. The oldest too. I'm going to be living in her home as soon as someone gets their head out of their ass and lets me go. I have plans for that place." The man, he thought he said his name was Brooks something, said the house and its contents were not his to use or to sell. "Then who the hell did she leave it to? Tony? If that's what she did, I guess it's all right. Why are you shaking your head, no? There ain't no one else around that she can leave everything to. Unless she left it to my niece. And that ain't going to happen."

"I was only here to tell you that you were not mentioned in her will at all, Mr. Harold. I have spoken to your niece, Penny, as well as your other brother Tony on your mother's behalf." The man stood up. "Now, I do hope you have a safe life after this. I'm on—"

"You said you spoke to my brother and niece. If they didn't get it, then you're going to tell me who I have to kill to make sure I get it. That ain't fair, I tell you." The man only stood there, not saying a word. Nor did he give much away in his face. This wasn't a man he'd play cards against. "You have to tell me. That ain't right."

"Well, I have taken care of your mother's wishes, and that is all I've been hired to do, Mr. Harold." James told him to sit down and to answer his fucking questions. "As titillating as that sounds, I'm going to have to pass. I have other people I report to, and I'm going to go back to my office. You have yourself a lovely day."

The man just left. No matter how many threats James tossed at the little fucker, he just kept going to the door like he was on some kind of happy trip and wasn't letting anyone take his buzz away. After tossing everything around the cell that wasn't screwed down, James sat down.

on the floor and thought about what it meant for him not to have his mom's house.

"It means a whole lot of shit, that's what it means." He usually spoke to himself and didn't even mind answering his own questions. It was about the only way he could get anyone to agree with him. "Fuckers. I'm going to figure it out too. See if I don't. Whoever got my mom's house, they'd better be making their will out, so I get it this time. I swear, they're going to be dead when I get to them."

Smiling to himself, he knew he didn't usually make that much sense when he was pissed off. Like today. Damn it all to fuck and back. Why didn't Emmie just give him the money out of his own mom's account? It wasn't like she was going to spend any of it. Not to mention, he thought there might be laws about that when you were the bank manager—fat lot of good that had done them all.

"Wouldn't even give over the keys to us so we could get us some ready cash. What sort of person does that sort of shit to their own brothers and their friends?" He asked Dutch about it. "You ever figure out where your sister hides her keys when she leaves work? I'm telling you, Dutch, we sure could make a lot of dough if she was just to accidentally leave them out someplace."

"She don't even tell me where she lives no more." Now that was cold, he thought. "You know where your niece is living now?"

"Nah, but then I don't really care so long as she's not fucking living with me. Did I tell you I tried to get her to get her ass in the house and fix me some dinner? She told me no. I tell you, Dutch, we got the worst of the worst of women in our families." Dutch agreed with him. "When I get out of here, I'm going to not only make sure Penny knows who's boss, but I'll also make sure she marries you. There ain't no reason whatsoever that she should be telling you no after leading you around for so long. Just like her to up and tell you no after you already told her you're a good catch for her."

While James didn't think Dutch was such a good catch, he did like the man. And then after the marriage, they'd be related for real. They'd be like brothers. That alone should have made Penny sit up and take notice of who she was getting married to. The Donnelly's were about as close to family as they could get.

"I've been thinking on something. I heard that guy telling you that your mom didn't put you in her will. Then he told you he talked to your niece and brother. You don't think she might have left it to me, do you? I mean, we was always at her house. And I didn't hit her around like I did my own mom when she was living." He asked him why the man didn't tell him when he was there. "I don't know that. You might be as right as rain about that part. I didn't think on that. Oh well. You should be getting out of here soon anyway, right?"

"I don't know when. They didn't tell me when they brought me in here on some trumped-up charges from the bank. I'm telling you right now, Dutch, that sister of yours is getting uppity. Not only that, I think she has this thing in her head that we're beneath her. When we all know that ain't even close to being true." Dutch pointed out how she was the bank manager. "The only thing I can say about that is, they must have been desperate to fill the spot. Not to mention, they got rules about hiring women to do a man's job. Why, I'm betting right now the people that run that bank are pissed off on account of how I was treated in there."

He and Dutch talked through the rest of the afternoon well into the night. When the lights went out, James laid on his bed and thought about the things he was going to be doing when he got into his mom's house. There was still plenty in the place that he could sell off. But the big television she'd just got, that was going to be in his bedroom.

James thought about Tony. He was about as stupid as stupid came when it came to anything. He didn't know from minute to minute what a person was talking about. No matter how many times he'd hit him upside the head to try and knock some sense into him, it didn't seem to stick. He often wondered if their mom had dropped him on his head a lot when he was a baby.

Tony couldn't be depended on for much in the way of going out on some robbery either. He'd have his part in the jobs they did told to him about fifty times, then he'd still mess it up. Now he wished that when Penny was little, he'd not killed her mom and brought the kid home for his brother. It was like the two of them didn't have a brain cell between them when Penny was a baby.

But she'd gotten smart. Not only did she finish up her schooling, but she went on to college. Why she'd done that, James didn't have a clue. What good was it to have smarts when all you were going to be good for was fucking? Not that he ever wanted to have sex with his niece, but that was what others around him had said.

He heard the woman down the hallway, talking again. The cops had told him she talked to herself all the time. She sure was giving herself a piece of her mind. He doubted she could have afforded to give up too much. He thought she was off her rocker. She was going on about her being some kind of adding machine or something like that. James wanted to tell her to shut her trap, but he knew that would just set her off to be louder.

"Hey, James. You awake?" He told Dutch he was. "I been thinking about what that lawyer said. He only told you that he talked to your niece and brother. He didn't say they weren't mentioned in the will. Just that he talked to them. Do you suppose your mom gave her house to your niece?"

That had him sitting up on his cot. "You thinking that or wishing it, Dutch? I mean, that would mean the house belongs to you when you marry up with Penny."

"I didn't think of that either. But I will tell you this—if that's what is going on, you know you always got a home with me. Even if Penny don't care for it, you know you can live with me for as long as you want." He told Dutch that was nice of him. "Like you said, we're going to be like brothers soon enough. There ain't no reason at all you should be out that house. It's not the best in the neighborhood, but it's big enough for us three, don't you think?"

"How are you going to talk Penny into marrying you? I mean, she seemed dead set against it when she was at the house." He said he was thinking about knocking her up. After that, she'd have to marry him. "I don't know, Dutch. Women don't have to marry like they used to. Damn shame about that, but I don't think that's going to work."

He didn't point out that him trying to knock his niece up was going to cause him all kinds of shit. Penny might be a pain in the ass, but she was fucking good with that gun she was carrying around all the time now. She'd been sassy since she'd been hanging out with that fucking Emmie.

"I'll see about that." Both of them were quiet for a while. Then when Dutch started laughing, he asked him what was so funny. "Your niece, being fat with my kid. I was just thinking how I wasn't going to stop fucking her just because she'll look like the side of a cow."

"Dutch, I don't want to hear about you screwing my niece if it's all the same to you." That made him laugh harder. "You just get her married to you, and things will be just hunky-dory. No matter if she got my mom's house or not, she must be living someplace close to here. She sure was johnny on the spot when my mom died."

James tried to think if he'd ever been to Penny's house. He knew she had to be going someplace to live. He'd not seen her at his place for a while, not even at Grandpa Joe's house that he could see when he'd been there. He wished sometimes he'd been living with the old man rather than with his mom. She didn't take care of the house, or things, as well as the old man, did. Everything was spotless there.

It sure would be nice to have a maid to come around and pick up after him. There'd be other perks for her too. He'd fuck her whenever she got finished cleaning up for whoever was living with them. Also, he thought having someone to do his laundry, and other things around the house would be nothing to sneeze at.

Then he thought of Emmie. She wasn't too bad on the eyes. Skinny as fuck, but she had herself some nice titties. He thought if he could just fuck her, she'd want to hang out with him more and more. James sat up in the bed when something just hit him right between the eyes.

"Hey Dutch, what if I were to marry your sister? I mean, that would make us double related, don't you think? And the way Emmie and Penny get along, they'd surely see this as a great thing on account of them being sisters like for real."

Dutch didn't answer him, so he laid back down. The man was probably asleep.

Tomorrow he'd put out the word that he wanted to talk to Emmie. She might not come; he was aware of that.

He'd pissed her off something terrible when he'd been at the bank. James frowned. Now that he had a minute to think on it, she wasn't the least bit upset about him being arrested. Nor did she have that Bishop bastard let him stand up. Right then, he decided he didn't want to talk to her about the mess she'd made for him at the bank. Emmie seemed to think she was in charge or something.

There were gonna have to be rules when they were married. Like she'd be giving him the keys to the bank when he asked for them. Then there was the cooking and cleaning shit that had to be done. James figured Penny and Emmie would be good at keeping house for their husbands.

The more he thought about it, the more he liked the idea. Not just the fact that they'd have the house and all that came with it, but the girls had jobs. He and Dutch would have it on easy street. If he got her pregnant a couple of times, they could get one of those welfare cards his mom had always gotten. Steaks every night for dinner. Beer stocked up in the fridge. Christ, he should have thought of this shit years ago.

Being too excited to sleep well, he was nearly ready to leap on the person who brought him his breakfast. It took him a few minutes to get Dutch to answer him, and when he was surly to him, he thought about not telling him his fantastic idea. After he told him, Dutch didn't answer for a while and that sort of pissed him off. James told Dutch to stop ignoring him.

"I'm not ignoring you, dumbass. I'm thinking." James

asked him if he was hurting from that. "Don't be a cock sucker, James. I was thinking on about what you said about marrying my sister. I have some questions about that."

"Are you going to ask me if I can provide for her or some shit like that?" They both laughed. Dutch did ask him what he'd been thinking on. "Yes, I'd let you pop her when she needed it. Same with your wife, I'm thinking. They might learn not to be bitching to you and me as their husbands, but you know they're going to be pitching a fit at their brothers. Pop her all you want. So long as you don't touch her titties or her pussy. That's going to be all mine."

Both of them were laughing hard when they talked over the two cells between them. The woman at the other end was bitching again, and he could see that she was being taken out. While he didn't give a shit on why she was even in jail, he did wonder if her bitching about shit was going to put the judge in a bad mood for when he got there.

After shoving his tray out when he was finished with it, James laid back on the bed. He didn't really want to get hitched, but the benefits of being married to Emmie were too hard not to think about. She'd have to let him in the vault at her work, he thought. There wasn't any way she was going to tell him no without him knocking her around a bit. Hell, he thought, he might just demand she get him a copy of the keys so he'd be able to come and go as he pleased. Being married was going to have way more benefits than having a clean house. It was going to put money in his pockets all the time too.

"James Harold, get up and against the wall. You're seeing the judge today."

He stood up and got against the wall. He didn't fuck with these people, no matter how much they pissed him off.

By the time he was getting loaded up in the car they were transporting him in, he had to pee something terrible. It was their fault, he thought, for not reminding him to empty out before he left the jail. Now, he'd been told, he'd have to hold it. Like that was supposed to be something a grown man had to do.

The building was surrounded by people when they pulled up in front of it. James asked three times what was going on and never got an answer any of those times. There were even camera crews from stations he'd never heard of before. One of them, he noticed, had a license plate from way out west. He wondered what the hell was going on.

Getting into the building was a nightmare. There were, just like outside, people everywhere. He did kind of enjoy it when the people parted when he was led down the hall. He wondered if anyone thought of him as a dangerous criminal. That would be fantastic, he thought, if they were all here to see what sort of bail he was going to be getting.

There was going to be a wait, he was told by the three men with him. James told them again that he had to piss, but it didn't seem to bother them. If he wet his pants, he told one of them, he was going to make them clean it up.

All that got him was a cuff to the side of his head. Fuckers, every damned one of them.

"You can pee in a minute. I've got to be in there with you, Harold. You're aware of that, aren't you?" He asked the guy if he was going to hold his dick for him. "Sure, I will if I can find it. I heard from one of your victims that you don't have much to show for all your bragging."

"I'm not small, you fucking prick. I'll show you if you want." The man laughed, and James got pissed. Before he could say a word to the man, he was called to go into the courtroom. "You just saved your own life there."

"Are you threatening me, James? I surely hope you are." James told him he wasn't threatening him but making a promise. "That's perfect. You just threatened an officer of the law, dummy. Now we're going to have you at our nice jail for a few more days."

Fucking shit head. He had never learned to keep his mouth shut. And now here he was getting charged with shit while he was in the fucking jail. Would his luck ever change? He thought it would as soon as he got himself attached to Emmie. Then heads would roll, or he'd know the reason why.

Chapter 3

Wesley was just finishing up reading the instructions on cleaning the tractor when Penny joined him in the barn. He'd left before sun-up this morning and hadn't woken anyone in the house as he fixed himself something to eat and left the house. She asked him if she could talk to him.

"Sure. Just let me put this stuff away. I've never had equipment like this before. I don't want to come out here in the spring and find it's all been rusted through or something." She asked him if he thought that was going to happen. Wesley laughed a little. "No. I'm babbling. Making small talk for fear of you telling me that you guys are all moving out."

"No. We're not moving out. This is such a nice place I might not ever want to leave. But that's not what I wanted to talk to you about. Your mom, she came by yesterday when you were at the Sanford farm. Thank you for that, by the way. Giving me a list of places you'd be in the event that I needed you." He told her it was his pleasure. "Anyway, your mom came by and said she was going to make sure I was aware of the Thanksgiving schedule. I didn't know what she was talking about, but she handed me a list. I guess I'm to sign us up for some part of the meal that is going to be at Sawyer's home. Did you know anything about it?"

"I sort of did. I mean, I remember them talking about it the other night. I didn't really pay attention because I'd just put in a long day, and I figured someone would update me on it when it was time." He took the list when Penny held it out to him. "Okay. Now I remember. Sawyer and Raven were making the meat, and we were each to bring something we really like to the meal. We can either sign up for dessert, side dishes or a go along."

"Yeah, I saw that too. What is a go-along? I mean, I sort of have an idea what it is, but I don't know for sure." He told her. "Okay, that's what I thought. Things like drinks and butter that will go along with the meal. Do you cook?"

"I can if pressed. I know how to cook, but I don't enjoy it overly much. However, for this, I'll do it. I can make green beans with ham as a side." She told him she loved to cook. "Awesome. If you'd like to do this, then I'm all for it. What is it you can make?"

"Anything. I can do things from when I was living at home, comfort food. Or I can do something I have a recipe for. That is if I can have all the ingredients right in front of me." Wesley told her she could get whatever she wanted, and it would be in the kitchen for her. "Would you mind overly much if I started filling out the other parts of the house? I'm not saying it's something I'll do for sex."

"I don't know if you've realized this or not, but I'm not a person that bargains or demands that you do things in trade for sex. We'll make love when you're ready." She asked him if he'd be willing to wait that long. "Yes. I want you; I won't lie to you about that. In fact, I can't lie to you, not that I ever would, but I don't want you to hate me even before we get to fall in love."

"Do you think that is possible? For us to fall in love?" He told her he hoped so, that he was always hopeful for someone to love him. "You're a very strange man, Wesley. I have a feeling, however, that under that shield of just being an aw-shucks farmer, you have a side of you that can scare people if necessary. Do you have a beast inside of you?"

"Yes." Penny stared at him for several seconds before she only nodded and asked him what he wanted for dinner. Just like that, he thought, she was all right with him having another side of himself. "Dinner? I don't know. I mean, I've just been having sandwiches for the past three months while I got the crops in and the ground ready. By the way, Penny, are you all right with me being a farmer? I'll find another job if this isn't anything you'd be proud of telling people I do for a living."

She looked around the barn, and he did too. There were

things in here that were older than his dad, but he still used them. Dirt too, that was older than anyone around, spread out almost as smooth as the hardwood floor in the house. She turned to look at him.

"This is you. You're a farmer. Not only that, I think that taking even a little of this away from you would make you fade away." He thanked her. "There are a great many jobs out there that you could do that I know you'd do well. But this job, being a farmer, is one of the oldest and most fulfilling jobs there is, I believe. You just don't feed a family with this, Wesley, but an entire town. Even animals get something of what you've done here."

He kissed her on the cheek and thanked her again. When they both seemed embarrassed by the seriousness of the conversation, he decided to change the subject. But seeing her there, her cheeks all pink from the compliment, he had to turn away and look at what he'd been doing before she came in the barn.

"You're very beautiful. The first time I saw you, I was in awe of your beauty and poise. I didn't know you were my mate then. But sitting there, watching you and your grandda fixing things up so that his grandsons wouldn't bother you was— Well, it was the kindness you showed toward him. An elderly gentleman that had to make sure his own family didn't rob him blind."

"I love him." Wesley looked at her and told her it was much more than that. "He raised me; did you know that? I didn't know who my mom was, but I thought about her often. If it hadn't been for Grandpa Joe and Emmie, I don't think I would have survived my childhood. My dad wasn't so bad, not really, but Uncle James would get him into trouble a great deal."

"I don't know your uncle well, but I've seen your dad around town a few times. He seems very gentle." She told him she thought that as well. Then her uncle would get him to do things. "I'm sorry about that. It's rough when family forever takes advantage of someone. We don't have that in my family. I think it has a great deal to do with us being shifters."

"I've always loved your family. From afar." He laughed when she did. "You might not remember this, but your mom, she was forever sending things to Grandpa Joe's house for the three of us. Food. Blankets that she told him she didn't need. We both knew she was helping out an old couple raising a child. He loved that she didn't try and embarrass us in that way."

"My mom has the nicest way about her that makes her the talk of the town. A great many people benefit from us having fruit trees and a large garden. I try hard to follow in their footsteps now. If I have it and you need it, I want you to have it. The same with you, Penny. Whatever you want, I'm going to try my best to make sure you have it." She looked away again, and he could see her eyes were filling with tears. "I'm sorry. I don't know what I said to upset you, but I'm profoundly—"

"It's not so much what you said but that you'd actually

do what you're saying. You would give this all up, no matter how much it meant to you, just to satisfy me. No one, not in all my life, would have done something like that for me." She laughed a little. "They might well have said it, but they wouldn't have meant it. Not like you do."

He didn't know what to say to her on that, but did put out his hand for her to take should she wish. When she did, wrapping her much smaller one into his, Wesley felt like he could conquer the world with one hand tied behind his back.

"You've made me safe and secure. Things I've not felt in a long time." Wesley told Penny he would continue to do so because he wanted her to feel safe and secure. "Thank you, Wesley. You keep this up, and I'll be announcing to the world that I've fallen in love with you."

"I cannot wait for that day." He let her go when she pulled her hand out of his. She didn't leave him but walked to the other side of the barn to look at the things there. He cleaned the tractor the way the instructions recommended. When he was finished, he drove the tractor deeper into the barn and covered it with a tarp. "I never did this before about five years ago, covering the tractor. But I came out here once to check on things, and there were enough bird droppings on the seat that I vowed never to let that happen again."

The two of them worked in the barn together as he put the implements away. There were several pieces he'd not gotten to use this year but had good ideas on how he was going to work them into his next year of planting. They moved out into the sunshine just as someone pulled into the driveway.

He didn't know the person who got out of the truck, but that didn't stop him from being friendly to him. Wesley started to stand in front of Penny, so this person wouldn't approach her, but she moved toward the house on her own. Wesley watched her until she was inside before he turned to the man.

"May I help you?" The man asked if he was one of the Bishops. "I don't know who I am. Why don't you tell me why you're asking after them, and I'll let you know how you can find them."

"Fair enough. I was actually looking for Gunner. Do you know him?" He didn't even blink an eye as he reached for his brother to tell him someone was looking for him. "I guess that's not going to get me any information either. What if I told you I had money for the other man?"

Did he tell you his name yet? Wesley told Gunner he didn't. *Then don't tell him anything about me. I was painting here at the house if he wants to give you more than he is right now.*

"Are you speaking to your brother, Mr. Bishop? It would go a long way in me being able to finish up my job if you were to tell him someone is looking for him." He heard the front door open and saw the stranger put his hands in the air. Glancing quickly at the front of his home, he had to look a second time to see Penny standing there with a gun pointed at the man. "I meant no harm in coming here."

"Sure, you didn't. Then why are you not telling him your name? For that matter, why are you being all cagy about why you're looking for Gunner Bishop? Who are you?" The man told her, and he relayed the information to Gunner. "Why are you hunting Mr. Bishop? You'd better be more forthcoming here, or you're going to lose a part of your body, buddy. I'm not in any kind of mood to fuck around with people today."

"As I said, my name is Conway Baxter. I'm here representing a firm that would like to hire Mr. Gunner as a consultant on a movie set. But perhaps I've come for the wrong Bishop. You seem to be able to handle yourself better than most men I know." Penny didn't lower her gun, nor did she smile at the man's attempt at a joke. He did look at Wesley. "I guess here in Ohio, you don't have much of a sense of humor when you have visitors coming all the way across the country to speak to someone."

"As you can see, my wife is very good at keeping strangers at bay. I'm to tell you from Gunner that he's not interested in whatever you want from him. He said if you come around again, he will let my wife take you to task. If you don't think she could do that, you stay where you're standing, and she'll prove it." The man shook his head and got back into his car. "The highway should be less busy this time of the morning. Be on your way, or else I'll call out the troops. They have less of a sense of humor than we do."

After the man left, having taken a picture of his license plate, Wesley turned to see that Penny was sitting down on the steps leading up to the front door with her head between her legs. He sat down next to her, rubbing his hand up and down her back as she breathed heavily in and out.

"Thank you for that." She glanced at him from her position. "Seriously. I don't know what he wanted, nor did he seem all that forthcoming about it. I think he thought I was going to be a pushover. I am, don't get me wrong, but you proved to him not to fuck with us."

"I thought you'd be mad that I came out here with a gun." He asked her why. "I haven't any idea. Maybe I thought you'd be pissed because I was protecting you."

Wesley laughed. "Anytime you think I need protecting, you go right ahead and do it. I can be too friendly at times. I think it's sort of the middle child thing. I trust way too much in people."

She laughed with him as she sat up straighter. "I think I've told you this before, but you're very strange, Wesley Bishop." He laughed and stood up. "I was just going to suggest that we have some lunch and head to town. I have to see about having my loom brought here. If you don't mind."

"Loom?" He laughed before she could explain. "When your grandda told me you wove, I just assumed it was baskets or something. I didn't even consider you were looming things. That's wonderful. If you'd like to have it in one of the rooms, that's good. Or there is another insulated building here on the property, with heat and air."

"That would be perfect." They wandered to the back of the house where the second building was. "I could even have trucks back here when I have a shipment to go out. This is perfect."

"We'll have to put in a walkway for you. I wouldn't want to be stepping in the wet grass or snow to go to work." He was also thinking about how she needed a truck to back into the building to have a shipment go out. "You must be in high demand."

"Sort of. I have an online presence that sells well. Also, there are a few stores across the world that carries my things. I'm not a millionaire by any sense of the word, but I am able to support myself. Grandpa was very proud of my ability to do that, and told me so." Wesley told her he was proud of her too. "Yes, well, it was easy to do once I got the hang of it, and I can make a good profit out of what I make, so I don't have to work myself to death in order to pay my rent someplace. But this place here? Wow, I could really spread out. Something I've not been able to do."

As they made their way into the house, Penny was telling him about how she'd made a great many of the rugs and throws in her home. Grandda had a lot of them as well. As soon as they were seated, Mr. Joe, as well as Emmie, joined them. She told them about her visit with her brother yesterday.

~*~

Raven made sure her mother could see her today. This was the sentencing phase of for her mother, and Raven wanted to be front and center when she was sent away. Even her dad and the rest of the Bishop family were there. She had a feeling they were just as excited to hear the news as she was.

When her mom was bought out of the backroom, Raven could tell someone had tried to clean her up a little. The dress she had on was a little big on her, but that wasn't what shocked her the most. It was her mom's face and hair, neither of which were done up, as Jane, her mother's real name used to call getting ready to face the world.

"All rise." When they were seated again, she noticed her mother was still standing and glaring at the line of people Raven was with. Mostly, Raven thought she was looking at her dad. "Ms. Stipple, you need to have a seat so we can get on with this sentencing."

"They're here." The judge told her he could see them. "Since they're here, they can pay whatever fine you think I'm supposed to owe for this ridiculous brouhaha and let me go home."

"Ms. Stipple, there isn't going to be bail for you. That boat already set sail. We're here today to tell you how long you're going to be spending in prison." She told the judge her name was Addington. "We've also established that it's not. Will you please sit down? Good lord, you've been nothing but a pain in my— I said to sit down."

Mother did, but she bounced back up in seconds. Finally, she turned to them again and called out her dad. Her too, but Dad was the one that stood up. Mother asked him what the hell he was wearing.

"Jeans and a nice shirt. We're going out to celebrate after this is over, and I wanted to be comfortable. Why do you care what I have on?" She told him he looked cheap. "No, I think that would be what you look like, Jane. I'm comfy, you're a pain in the ass."

"You'll have to change before we celebrate. And I do hope you're not taking me to someplace cheap for dinner. I want a nice steak and all the trimmings. I think I can have a good solid meal tonight, don't you?" He told her she'd not been invited. "Well, that's just rude. Why would you want to celebrate me getting out and coming home, to *my* home, if I've not been invited? Don't bring that little bastard with you either. I'll not have that monster of Raven's messing up my celebration."

"You do know that because you lied on just about everything during our horrible life together, Raven is also a bastard." Mother totally ignored him to talk about her. "She's here, Jane. If you have something to say to her, why don't you say it to her face?"

Raven stood up then, proud of the fact she was showing a great deal and that her mother couldn't help but notice. Rubbing her hands over her baby she carried, Raven smiled when her mother asked her why she'd not gotten rid of it as she'd told her to.

"You might find this a little hard to believe, but I no longer do what you tell me." Mother told her she'd never done anything she'd told her to do. "That's true too. For your information, Sawyer has adopted Molly, and now she's a Bishop. This baby will be as well."

"I don't care what you put on its headstone. I want you to get rid of it. I'm much too young to be a grandmother. I told you that when you shit out that other monster."

It hurt her in ways that she couldn't imagine when her mother said things like that about her children. When Sawyer took her hand into his and Dad the other, she felt a renewed strength that she'd felt every day since she'd been married. Glaring at her mother just once more, she sat down with her family.

"Ms. Stipple. Will you please sit down and shut up?" She told him she wasn't finished. "Well, I've had more than enough. I have your sentencing right here, and I'm going to read it off to you."

"You're just wasting your time. I know they have the money to bail me out. Tell them to get on the stick so I can get away from the nasty reprobates that are locked up." He told her the only place she was going to was to prison. "For what? For trying to keep my name in good standing? For making sure the good name of Addington is now and will forever be a name that means something? Get that stick out of your ass and just tell them how much you're going to make them pay for me being locked up for the last several months. Not too extravagant—I do have to redo my home when I get back there. I just can't imagine what sorts of things have been done to my home since I have been taking time away from it."

"Ms. Jane Stipple, this court has found you guilty on all counts brought before you. A list of them will be handed to you once you are in the safe hands of the prison you're going to be sent to. Your sentencing is seven hundred years—that is one hundred years for each death you caused for your family. An additional six hundred years for the six people you murdered that we're aware of. Also, you are never going to be eligible for parole, nor will you be able to leave the prison on good behavior. Not that I think you could do that anyway. Behaving doesn't seem to be anything that you're good at."

"Are you quite finished?" He told her she would be taken to the prison as soon as the paperwork was filed. "Whatever. Have you decided on a bail amount yet?"

"Did you hear what I told you?" She said she had, but it didn't pertain to her. "Why the hell not? Please, tell me why your sentencing isn't something you should have?"

"Because, as I know I have pointed out to you on several occasions, Addingtons don't do prison terms. Not that I think I should do one in the first place. The name Addington is pure, and it's a good solid name. Made more so by my own hard work. Why, before I was one of the elite, the name was rubbish. Just look how my husband is dressed. Garbage. I tell you right now, I'm not going to allow you to spoil things for me, so I have to sue you for having me locked up all this time."

The judge looked at them. He finally smiled and looked around the room at the crowds of people that had shown up today. The verdict had been guilty on all crimes, even the one where she'd threatened the officer that had arrested her at the country club. Her mother, because she'd been found mentally competent to stand trial, would be in a prison lockdown for the rest of her life.

"Also, how is it you expect me to take you seriously for telling me I have to serve seven hundred years? I'm not sure where you learned your addition, but I doubt anyone in their right mind would think you were serious." She looked at them, then back at the judge. "Unless this is you showing off for me. I hate to tell you this, but you're as beneath me as everyone in this room is. Nice try, but I'm not going to help you up the ladder of the rich. You'll have to do that on your own."

When the judge told the police to take her away, Mother was still screaming about how she wasn't going to help him. With what, that wasn't clear, but she did tell him he'd rot in hell over his treatment of her. The judge looked around the room before clearing his throat and speaking.

"Never have I seen anything quite like I did today. That's not true. I've not seen anything like this in all my career as a judge. That woman would try a saint and have him questioning his faith." He shook his head. "It is my duty to tell you that she will not be allowed visitors for the first several months. That way, they can get her settled in her new home and hopefully, doubtful I'm thinking, have her realize she's there for the rest of her life, and never coming out again."

Dad stood up to address the judge before they left. "Your Honor, we, none of us, have any intentions of visiting her at all. As far as we're concerned, the family and I have written her out of our lives." The judge told him that was probably for the best. "Also, Your Honor, I did want to thank you for fast-tracking my paperwork for my daughter and myself. You've no idea how much easier you've made it for us to move on from this."

"It was my pleasure." He smiled at him. "Mr. Addington, I do hope you find yourself happiness after all this. I have been by the Bishop home a few times and have seen you outside with your young granddaughter. There is nothing like grandchildren to bring out the best of any terrible situation."

"I agree, sir. More so than you can ever imagine, I agree with that. And now I'm going to be a grandda again. The others in this family have adopted me as well, calling me their grandda right along with the others. I think I've come out on top with this, sir. I cannot think of anything I'd rather have than what I have right here and in the future."

Dad asked if he could approach the bench. When he was there, he reached for and was given the hand of the man who had put up with her mother for the last several months. While she couldn't hear everything that was being said, Raven did get most of it. Dad was thanking the man and then invited him over for dinner one night. Just as two old men, Dad told him, who could compare pictures of their grandchildren. The judge agreed.

Raven was glad to be finished with all this. She was also glad she'd not brought her daughter with her. It would have hurt her again to hear the things her grandmother said about her. Grandma looked relieved as well like a burden had been lifted from her shoulders. Raven thought she might be the one with the most to be happy with. Grandma had been around from the beginning of Jane's terror.

"I was thinking that tomorrow you and I, with the rest of the women, go on a shopping spree. I need to get my granddaughter something for being my granddaughter, as well as something for the new one." Raven pointed out that she'd given her a great deal, and that her new baby wasn't going to need anything more until he reached college age. "Whatever it is, it'll have plenty for college too. I might even have to put a little aside for him to have when he gets there. Is this little person you're carrying around a boy, Raven?"

"You have to wait like the rest of the family does. Though I think they might know already." Grandma told her it wasn't fair that they knew before she did. "Yes, but you're going to be there with us when I give birth, so you can't complain too much. Along with Sippy."

"I love that woman too. She's a hoot when she gets on a roll." The two of them, Sawyer's mom and her grandma, had been seen with their heads together a great deal since she'd married Sawyer. "All right. I guess I can live with that. But you remember what I told you. You and I, we're going to have a good time once this one is born. You'll need me to keep you on your toes."

"Grandma, I'm not sure if you realize this or not, but you keep all of us on our toes." Grandma was laughing when she left her standing there. Sawyer wrapped his arms around her from behind. "I think we're going to have some major issues about babysitting when this one is born."

"I think you might be right on that." He turned her around and kissed her, then leaned down to kiss her belly. "I love all of you. I think we should swing by the school and get Molly so she can celebrate too. I've already texted her about the verdict. Also, I sent her a few short recordings of Jane while I was at it."

Those two. It was funny when people that didn't know the family would say how much Holly looked like her father. Sawyer would puff out his chest like he'd invented children. The man was a wonder, she'd give him that. And Raven loved him with all she was.

Chapter 4

Gunner had the entire hotel room scanned within an hour after he entered the room. Even after hanging cameras in the two-room suite, he was still alone to do what he'd come here for. To figure out who and what Conway Baxter was.

There were things lying about the room, all misleaders, every bit of it staged, from the manuscript to the contract that was neatly laid out with a hotel pen next to it. There were two suits hanging in the closet — shirts in the drawers. There wouldn't be a single hair or DNA on any of it. Everything he'd hung or put away, Conway would have only just purchased it. Or the people he was working for had given the man what he needed.

Standing back, Gunner eyed the carpet and found the piece he'd been looking for. The rug had been moved — about an inch, not much more. When he did the same, tossing back the large area rug, he found the man's hidey hole. Pulling up the two boards that had also been moved, he found the large case and pulled it from the area that was the floor in this room and the ceiling of the one below it.

The lock on the case was complicated. Instead of fucking around with trying to get it open that way, he removed the hinges from the back and got into it from behind. People didn't realize that when they locked something up, they should make sure the hinges were sealed within the case, or they might as well leave it unlocked.

There were several passports, all of them with the same picture on them. But the names were different. Some of the passports were from other countries. He removed all of them and put them into a large envelope.

Next, there was money. Gunner thought that there was at least seven thousand dollars in the case, all US money. He had a feeling that should the man be driving anything but a rental, there would be other cases with money in that as well to swap out. He would also bet this money would be clean. No prints or DNA to be found here either. It was what his team called sterile money.

Gathering up all the money, he put it in another envelope. Just as he was pulling out the handguns, his handler and partner in this, Janice, contacted him. She was laughing, so he stretched out his shoulders and continued working.

I had no idea how boring it could be watching someone eat

their breakfast. Not to mention, he's putting enough catsup on his eggs to make me sick. Christ, who the hell does that to their breakfast? He laughed but didn't answer her. *I was just wondering if you found anything. I'm hoping so. This bastard needs to be arrested for his eating habits.*

I've found his passports, as well as some sterile money. Gunner knew she'd understand what that meant. She'd been in the business as long as he had, and they'd worked together for a long time. Working with just her, however, was a great deal more fun than he'd thought it would be. *I'm still searching. Cameras are up and running too. You should be able to see something now.*

Hang on. He knew she was frustrated over this. Doing a search on the name Conway Baxter hadn't gotten her anything but a dead end. Whatever this guy was up to, it wasn't for him to consult on a movie. *I got it. I can see you're on the floor. This is a nice setup. Where did you get this? I know you didn't get this kind of pictures from the ones I gave you.*

It's the ones you gave me, only I was able to tweak them a little. She asked if he'd do that for the rest of her stash. *I can. I'll show you how to do it too.*

Picking a few things out of his pocket, Gunner tested the walls. *Is that a stud finder you're using?* He said it was, but again, he'd tweaked it. *What are you looking for? You don't think he pulled out the walls and hid things there, do you?*

The stud finder would find any kind of metal. It would beep slowly if it were a little like you'd get from wiring or even some copper plumbing. But it would go off like a siren if it found a great deal of it. Like it was doing now.

Well, I'll be damned. He did take out a wall. He didn't bother telling Janice he told her so. She'd not think it was funny at all. Behind the wall that was neatly hidden behind the dresser and mirror set, he found six long-range rifles, two more handguns, as well as enough ammo to have a nice shoot out if he was trapped. *You do know that now this is my job, don't you? I mean, that's a shit ton of firepower. Do you suppose he was going to shoot you to have you work with him?* Janice laughed.

Janice, do you suppose he's here for something other than just getting me to work with him on a studio set? I'm kinda sad about that. She asked him what he thought was going on. Instead of answering her, he pulled out the file that was in the walls, too, with his name and picture on the front of it. He held it up to one of the cameras he'd just installed. *I think it's time you and I traded places.*

All right. He's not even close to being finished with his breakfast, so you'll have time to come here, and then I'll head over there. He told her what he'd done here. *All right. I'm going to have to have the room cleaned and emptied. Also, the guns will go with me. Good luck getting anything from him.*

Thanks. That was all he said. Gunner didn't tell her about the woman working with him. She had no name that Gunner would share. Her fingerprints had, like his, been burnt off a decade ago. His sometimes bed mate and always friend was dressed as one of the cleaning ladies. The weapons in her cart were there if you knew where to look. *You can do the clean up after I get there, however. I need to read over the paperwork with you to make sure we both have our asses covered when your boss comes to town.*

I understand. She probably would more than anyone. *All right. I'll wait here for you to come in. The staff here is all my men, as are the patrons. If the shit hits the fan, your ass is covered. All right?* He thanked her as he moved out of the room. With a single nod to "Nancy," he knew that no one would enter the room while he and Janice traded places. He wasn't going to go to her table, the one she'd been observing Baxter from all morning. No, Gunner was going to sit with the man and tell him what was about to happen. And plenty of shit was going to hit the fan. It just wasn't going to be Gunner's.

Janice had been assigned to work with him on several other cases since he'd been recruited in the army. He'd not cared for her at first. It wasn't that she wasn't good at her job—she was the best, he thought. But he thought her too pretty, too much of a distraction when she was around, not to him, but to the other people, men mostly, that he would work with. As it turned out, her looks had saved his life a few times.

Gunner hadn't told his family that he was still a service man. Nor had he told them he'd been killing people that fucked with the country for a very long time. He wasn't a hitman, a person that he knew for a fact the government employed. No, he was a person that would go in and "un-stir" up shit when it got out of hand. He had to laugh when the people he worked for called him the calm before the storm man. It either got calm when he arrived, or he would rain a storm over the situation where not one person was left standing but himself. He could also blend in and get out of any country in the world. Gunner was a ghost. No one saw him but felt the effects of his visit long after whatever had been going on was over.

Sitting down across from Baxter, he drank down the glass of tea he'd picked up from the table Baxter was sitting at. After setting the empty glass down on the table, Gunner pulled out his gun and laid it on the table between the two of them. Baxter started to reach into his own pockets.

"You pull anything but a tissue from your pocket, it's going to be a very messy clean up in here." Baxter stopped moving. "I want you to lay both your hands on the table with your fingers spread out."

The man complied but didn't want to. That was another thing Gunner could do well—make people do what he wanted them to do unless they were a leader or something akin to a leader in other shifter categories. But he still got what he wanted in the end.

"Why are you here? And if you lie to me or decide not to answer me, there will be consequences." The man bit through his lower lip, trying not to answer him. Gunner pulled his knife out of his boot and stabbed it into the top of the man's hand. The screams from the man didn't cause a ripple of interest from anyone in the restaurant. Just as he had wanted. "Let's try this again, shall we? Why are you here?"

Baxter, or whatever his name was, looked around the restaurant. Everyone was going about their business. Gunner made sure to wiggle the blade in his hand just enough to have him cry out. No one flinched when Baxter screamed again as Gunner pulled the knife out of his hand.

"I came here to have you consult on a movie that is being made." Gunner stabbed his other hand this time. "What the fuck is wrong with you? That fucking hurts."

"I know it does. However, I did tell you not to lie to me." The man tried again, telling Gunner that not only was he there for the very reason he said but that he had a contract back in his room. Gunner cut off the end of his middle finger. "Again, you don't want to lie to me."

The man was sweating bullets. Gunner knew he was also in a great deal of pain. Not that he cared. Gunner was being hunted by this man, and he was going to find out who had sent him and why.

"There is a contract in your room. I read it over while I was there. I'll pass, thanks. But you really fucked up by tearing into the walls of Mr. Hershel's room and pulling up the floor. How will he ever get that put back together where no one will try that again?" Gunner dumped the passports onto the table, unmindful of the blood staining them. "You see, I'm not nearly as stupid as you seem to think I am. Now, you're going to open your mouth and tell me who sent you here and why."

"They'll kill me and come after you again." Gunner

told the man he could live with that. "I have a family. Children."

"I guess it sucks to be related to you right now." Gunner had already made arrangements to have the man's family picked up, if he really had one, before he left the table. But it would only save them if he were willing to give over his real name. "Things are not going in your direction right now. Why don't we settle up by you telling me who you work for, and you can get someone to help you not bleed to death."

"I can't." This time, instead of stabbing him in the hand, Gunner removed a whole finger. The screams could be heard throughout the place, but not one person moved. He decided right there and then that he was going to have Janice help him with staff the next time he had to work with one. "Christ, I fucking loath you right now. It's a man by the name of Jackson. I don't know his first name, or even if that's his real name. He wanted you dead. Out of the picture, he told me. You fucked him over the last time he had a shipment coming in."

"You're very informed for someone that doesn't know his name." Gunner punched the man in the face with the butt of the blade he was holding. "Now, start from the top, and this is your very last chance to tell me what the fuck is going on."

Before Baxter could say a word, his head snapped backward when a hole about the size of a shot glass appeared in his forehead. Everyone in the restaurant, including Gunner, got on the floor. The shot had come from the direction of the bar, and that was where he was moving towards when the person opened fire again.

He had figured something like this would happen, that someone would take out Baxter before he could lead anyone back to where he was working from. What he'd not counted on was someone killing him in the restaurant. Reaching out to Janice, he was glad to know she'd not been taken out too.

Kill her.

That was all he needed to tell her about Nancy. Gunner knew that not only would Nancy be dead, but there wouldn't be a body left behind. It would be as if she never existed. When Janice reached back to tell him it was finished, he moved to the table next to the bar, glad now that he'd hidden things around the place in the event he ran into trouble.

The guns he had on him were still a part of his body, but he was going to use a knife first. Gunner reminded himself to pick up the one that had been left on the table and stood up. The bartender, the one that had been behind the bar when he came in, was reloading his gun—a rookie mistake.

"You never reload when the perp is still around. You should have brought several weapons with you. Since there won't be a next time for you, I'll just tell you that your boss is dead too."

The knife landed deep in his throat. Even if he were

to manage to pull it out, he'd be dead before any kind of medical team could save him. The knife was not just in his neck, but it was also holding him up by being stuck in the wall behind him.

Gunner looked around at the carnage that had been caused. Most all the tables were tipped over. Those that weren't broken were full of holes. The chairs were in bad shape too. Having been used as a shield, they didn't offer up much in the way of protection, he noticed as he walked around the room.

Picking up his knife, he looked over the body of Baxter. Just as he was pulling out the man's wallet, Janice spoke to him again. He paused in opening the wallet when she laughed.

Little Ms. Nancy has a purse full of identifications on her. She must have thought she was actually going to get out of this upright. It says here that her name is Margie Sweet. The man you're with there is— Wait, she has two identifications here. One named Billy Hartman. The other, the younger of the two, is Wendler Parks. He said they were both dead; at least he thought so. *Yeah, probably. When we meet up, we'll compare notes. Baxter tell you what was going on?*

He opened the wallet up and took the cash out of it. No credit cards, no pictures, just the cash. Gunner told her what he'd found so far. Tearing the wallet into pieces to find if there might be something else, he was disappointed to find nothing but another hundred bucks hidden behind the picture area. Then he checked the man's pockets. Not finding much more in his pants, he searched his jacket pockets.

I have a picture of me standing somewhere in a desert area. Doesn't really narrow it down, but it's me. He continued his search. *I'm going to check out the bartender who killed Hartman. Hopefully, we can nip this in the bud before anyone else comes around.*

Clean up is here. I'm going to let them do their job. Before I forget to tell you, the deed to this hotel has been changed. It was a good idea for you to buy it outright so that you could come and change things around as you needed them. You're a smart cookie. Anyone ever point that out to you? Anyway, I went by the courthouse earlier this morning to take your name off and put in the name you use when you don't want anyone to find you. That's a wonderful idea, by the way. I'd never think to look for you under Slaughterhouse Bakery. No one will ever know we've been here. He thanked her. *I'm coming to you – back door. There isn't any point in advertising that people are going in and out of the restaurant.*

He was sitting behind the bar when Janice came into the place. She sat at the bar when he stood up and poured her a drink, a full glass of whiskey. He had a glass of water. Handing her what he'd found behind the bar and on the kid, she told him the younger man was Parks, and the other man was Hartman. The notes he found were about him, very little as it turned out, but they'd known enough to find him in Ohio.

"This is pretty cut and dried. Whose name is this, do

you know?" He told her he did. "I'm guessing you're going to have to have another clean up on aisle four then, huh?"

"Perhaps. If you were to read over the entire thing, you'd see that the person who sent them after me didn't have much to go on either. I especially like the part where he calls me a fart in the wind. Do you suppose he really thought that, or did he think of himself as a funny guy?" She laughed with him. "It's going to take me a few days to find Mr. Swartz. When I do, you want to make some extra cash?"

"You know I'll go with you anywhere." She sat there for a little while, sipping her second glass of whiskey. "No, I can't go with you on another one of these trips. I'm getting too old for this shit, Gunner. I want to retire. Sit on a fucking beach someplace and not have to worry that the next time I start my car, it might blow me to shit. When I take a lover, I want it to be a fun filled night with breakfast in bed the next morning. Not a quickie with someone in a dark alley. You're a good fuck, Gunner, the best I've ever had, but I'm wanting more than a big cock from a man that has less idea of commitment than I do. I'm finished."

"I'll have to kill you. You're aware of that, aren't you?" She nodded. "Pick a body out, and we'll make sure they find you dead someplace. Otherwise, this will come back and do more to you than just put a bomb up your ass."

"Thanks, Gunner." She grinned at him. "When you find a mate, I'm hoping she fills your heart and makes you into the best man in the world."

"Fuck you."

They did what was necessary for her to be found dead over the next few days. He didn't think she'd be able to stay out of this completely, but he was going to give her the best start he could. No one would be able to hunt her down again. More than likely, he wouldn't be able to find her either.

Neither one of them had any kind of records on file that they'd be able to compare a dead body to. Just putting what Janice had on her on the body was all they'd have. He knew for sure that their dental records, DNA, prints, and anything else that would be used for identification wouldn't be found. The two of them really were ghosts.

~*~

Wesley was putting away the tools he'd used that morning to fix a door in the house when he heard screaming. Rushing out into the yard, he was headed to the house when Penny came out the back door with her hand held above her head. Her blouse had blood on it. So did her face. Racing to her, she was ready to run him down when he grabbed her and held her to his body.

"Calm down." He knew he was harsh in his tone, but he couldn't understand what she was screaming about. Taking her hand that was covered in blood, he saw that she'd cut her wrist badly. "I need to seal this for you. All right? Then you're going to tell me what you did to cut yourself this way."

"All right." He opened up the lengthwise cut in her

wrist and licked it there. Then when the bleeding was almost stopped, he licked it again just to be sure. Closing up the wound, then with his hands, he sealed it as well. Then he held her. "I was cutting up vegetables that your mom gave me. I wasn't paying attention to what I was doing. The television was on, and something on there scared me. That was when the knife slipped."

Wesley felt like his heart was going to explode in his chest. It was getting better, but he'd been terrified something had happened to her. Lifting her chin up to see into her eyes, she told him she was sorry she'd panicked.

"You did the right thing, Penny. Had you not found me, you would have bled to death. What scared you on the television?" When she told him, Wesley asked her what had scared her about Butch. "You know, now that I think about it, I've never met him. Where has he been all this time?"

"He was coming out of a big house that the news people were telling a story in front of. I was only half paying attention when I saw Emmie's brother. Butch was just standing there like he was confused about how he'd gotten there. I guess there was some kind of murder-suicide in the house." Wesley was going to see if he could get some information on the man. No one seemed to talk about him much. "You don't have on a shirt."

He just glanced down at himself as he thought about Butch. "Yes. It gets really hot in the barn when I'm working. I didn't know some maniac was going to come out of the house screaming bloody murder." He lifted her chin up and looked at her face. "Why is me being shirtless bothering you?"

"Bothering me? I don't think that would be the word I'd use." He nearly fell backward when she licked his nipple then bit down on it gently. "Now, if you were to ask me if it was getting me all hot and bothered, then yes, that would be the words I'd use."

He picked her up, and she giggled. Taking her back into the barn, he shoved her up against the wall and tore her clothing off her. While she worked on the belt and zipper on his pants, he was taking her breast to his mouth. Christ, the need to have her came over him like an electrical storm.

"Hurry." He told her he was trying. "You have too many clothes on. Why are you even wearing a belt?" He jerked if off his pants. Penny laughed again. "This is going to be quick and dirty, isn't it?"

"Yes." He slammed his cock into her, and she screamed out her release. Wanting to make it last at least a second or two longer, he tried to slow down, but she wasn't having it. As soon as his cock filled, his balls aching to release, she bit down on his shoulder hard enough to make him see stars and for his release to take him. "You're not going to enjoy this much if you don't let me have my fun."

"Oh Wesley, I'm enjoying myself so much right now that I'm going to come again." Her neck was borne to him as she threw back her head in submission. The need to bite her, to taste of her hot spicy blood, made his cock fill again.

"Again. I need to come again."

Biting her, just tasting her at her richest point, he nearly dropped the two of them to the ground when she came with him. Nothing could have prepared him for what happened between them. He was sure that while he'd not ask anyone about it, this making love with his mate was one for the books. Christ, he was so in love with her that he could have taken out an ad in every paper in the world, and it wouldn't have been enough.

It was quick, their coupling. Coming three times himself made him weak in the knees, his breaths coming out in short puffs of air. Never in all of his life had he ever had such a reaction to a woman. He doubted he ever would again. Penny was his mate.

Holding her up by pressing her to the wall, Wesley touched her as much as he could. Her skin was cooling off. A breeze into the barn also had her sprinkled in dust. Kissing her neck where he had bitten her, Penny moaned twice before she pulled his head back by his hair.

"Stop teasing me. You have no idea— Well, perhaps you do have an idea about how I'm feeling right now." He kissed her before telling her some of the feelings he was having. "Do you really love me?"

"Yes. I have for some time, but I didn't tell you because you seemed so determined to keep me at arm's length." She looked down at the two of them, still connected in the most intimate way. "Okay, maybe not that far away, but you were making sure there were people around when we were in a room together. I thought I smelled or something."

"No. *Yes*, you do smell. It was all I could do not to jump you every time you came into the house after working outside all day. Were you by chance avoiding me?" He didn't even try and deny it. Wesley had been avoiding her. "I see. Boy, were we at cross purposes. I guess we could have been fucking around all along if not for me trying my best to keep away from you. I'm sorry."

"Don't be. This was great." He held her up a little more, to have her mouth right where he wanted it. "I love you, Penny Bishop. More and more with every beat of my heart. And anytime you want to jump me, you don't have to cut yourself. Please, don't do that again." She told him she wouldn't. "Now, tell me why you were so afraid when you saw Butch on television. Do you think he was the one that murdered those people? I didn't even know he was in Columbus."

"I don't know what I think, to be honest. Butch and Dutch are twins, did I tell you that?" He said he hadn't known that. "They're identical. But you'd never know that if you didn't just talk to them separately. They're so different; it's like looking at two people that look alike but are from different families."

"And what is it he does that is so different than Dutch?" She told him he would beat her up when he was near her. Steal from whoever had the money. "Sounds just like Dutch if you ask me. What else?"

"Dutch has killed people, and Butch, as far as I know,

hasn't." He let her down to the ground when she shivered. "Are you upset with me?"

"Good heavens, no. Why would you think that?" He handed her the shirt he'd taken off earlier when it got to be too hot. "I love you. I was just thinking about the differences between them. When you said that Butch hadn't killed anyone, how sure are you about that? For all you know, he might have fifty people in shallow graves around. I'm not being a smart ass here; I'm just trying to figure this out."

"I know. But I know because he told me that once." He looked at her skeptically. "No, seriously. He was telling me that when he said Dutch had killed a lot of people. That he was also going to kill me. That was about the time I started to carry a gun."

"Something that I've been meaning to ask you. Will you marry me, Penny? As soon as it can be arranged. I want you to be my wife. I'm in love with you." She stared at him, then told him the entire town thought they were already married. "Yes, my dad did do that, but it certainly was helpful when we found out his plans, right? All right, if that doesn't make you want to be my wife, it'll be harder for your relatives to marry you off if you're already married."

"Wow, that was.... You're strange, Wesley Bishop. And no matter the reasoning, I will marry you. As soon as it can be arranged." He did a little dance, and she laughed. "I will also require a ring from you. A pretty one. It doesn't have to be diamonds, but a pretty ring."

"You got it. Tomorrow morning we'll meet at the courthouse and get hitched. That'll be enough time for my family to get ready to welcome you into our big family." He kissed her again, telling her again that he loved her. "I will make you as happy as you do me with every breath I take."

When they were both dressed as well as they could be with what little they had left to wear, he walked with her into the house. He sent her off to their bedroom, hoping they'd be sharing it now, as he cleaned up the blood. There had been a great deal of it too.

"Hello." He looked at Gunner when he came into the room with him. Not a sound had been made, and he wondered just how many people he'd snuck up on the same way. "Don't think like that. Please. I'm home to stay."

"I know." Then he told him what Penny had told him. "How would I go about looking into this?"

"I'll do it." Wesley thanked him. He wasn't even sure how to go about looking into murders. "Wesley, your pants are buttoned wrong." Well, one more thing he was going to have to live down, he supposed. But he did fix his pants. Christ, two minutes more and— Wesley eyed his brother. "No. I stayed away when I heard her scream. I didn't see anything." He hoped not. Wesley would hate to have to tangle with his brother. He'd come out on the bottom, he knew it. Yes, he didn't want to tangle with his older brother.

"Tomorrow morning, meet us at the courthouse. Penny has agreed to marry me. I just have to find her a pretty ring. I wonder how I go about that." Gunner told him not to ask him, but Mom might be able to help. "I'll spring the wedding on her, then ask for help with a ring. She'll love it."

Chapter 5

The semi pulled up in front of the house. Penny remembered at the last minute that she didn't want to rush outside and get herself killed. Either of her brothers could be out there, and she didn't want to have to worry about being unarmed. Picking up her gun, which she carried all the time when not at home, she made her way out to the truck bearing the name of some rental company she'd heard of.

"I'm to tell you the code before I get out of the truck." She asked him what it was. "Seven lords a leaping. That's a good one, by the way. Usually, it's just a name or a number. This was fun. Can I get out now?"

"Sure, but you do know that if you come out of that truck with anything more than a clipboard, I'm going to blow a hole into your face." He just said, "Christ, lady," and slipped out of the truck. "Are you supposed to unload it?"

"No, ma'am. I was told you'd know to contact someone, and that there would be a lot of people here to help unload." She told him it was only a loom; how many did she need to unload that. "Loom? I have a loom, ma'am, but that's not all I have. There are boxes and boxes of stuff in there that I'm dropping off. All of it has your name on it."

Penny was confused but did reach out to talk to Wesley. He'd been called away early this morning to help with a field. His new stuff would need to be cleaned up again. Not that he minded, he told her. It kept him from taking her to bed again when they'd only just gotten it made — for the second time.

My cargo is here. He told her good. *Wait. Before you go and get all excited for me, there is more than just the loom on it that the driver says belongs to me. I didn't order anything but the loom to be brought here. I certainly didn't buy anything.*

Let me check on it. My brothers are here with me. Would you believe me if I told you we're harvesting pot? There are nearly two hundred acres of it planted with late corn. Christ, this is huge. She waited while he asked his brothers. The man driving the semi, Houston, was backing the big truck up to her barn. *It's all yours. Apparently, Raven found out that you loom things — what is that called? Anyway, she wanted you to be able to put some of your things in the shop in town that she's working on getting opened.*

I have my stuff all over the place now. Was she aware of that before she spent a fortune on material? She looked in the back of the truck when the doors were finally open. *Wesley, there are several hundred boxes on this sucker, all of it fabric that I can't afford. What the hell does she think I'm going to do with all this? Weave a blanket for the frigging world to cuddle into?*

Wesley laughed. She did as well, finding the humor in it finally. But it was just a little overwhelming to her.

I don't know. She's not here for me to ask. And when I reached out to her, she told me she was very busy right now. I guess she and her grandma have this business thing going on in the business district that they're helping out. Sawyer told me about two hundred people are going to be fired if they can't come to an agreement with the owner. Penny asked him where this was taking place. After he told her, Wesley asked her what she was going to do. *It might be better if I have some idea what's going on so that I bring enough money to bail you out.*

It's better if you don't know — that way, you have plausible deniability. However, I guess plans were made to have someone here to help with the unloading. Do you know anything about that? Wesley told her some of the pack had been paid to empty it out for her. She asked him to contact them for her. Closing the connection, she turned to Houston. "There are people coming here to help you unload."

Just after telling him where to put the loom, the only thing on the truck that she was aware of, she heard the first vehicle pull into their drive. Telling the man and his boys, he called them, to empty out what they could, she said she'd be back. The man, whatever his name was, laughed all the way to her back yard.

Penny had worked up a fine temper on her way to the company Raven was at with her grannie. As soon as she told the man at the front door who she was and why she was there, he got out of her way. She didn't know what she looked like to have him backing away from her, but she was glad she frightened at least one person. Barging into the office, Penny looked around and decided she wasn't nearly as pissed off as Raven was.

"Who are you?" The man she had pointed to stumbled out his name. "Mr. Holland, why are you even arguing with this woman? She'll tell you right to your face that she's never wrong when it comes to making a business deal. How the hell do you think she got so rich? It wasn't because she hasn't any business sense—you know that, don't you?"

"She wants to buy up my company and disband it." She looked at Holly, who explained. "That's what they're saying now. That they have no intentions of selling it off in pieces, but I know better. I've been around a lot longer than she has."

"Hello, Penny. Mr. Holland isn't going to meet payroll this week. He was only able to pay everyone last week because a large order was put into his company for one of the other ten products they make for her. But now that he's paid his people, there isn't any money for him to buy the product needed to make the order." She asked Raven, who was explaining all this if she was going to keep the business open. "Most of it, yes. But there are parts of this company that haven't shown a profit in over twenty years. Twenty years of draining the company of funds trying to make it sell. One product, in particular, is going to have to be cut out altogether. There isn't any retooling it at this point. He started making and selling it because his wife thought it would be a good seller. It wasn't. It never will be either. No one has any use for a device to play music when everyone and their brother has a cell phone."

"Okay." She turned to Mr. Holland. "You're an idiot. If I didn't know for a fact that hitting you over the head would only hurt my hand, that is what I'd do. Why are you even worrying about what she's going to do with your company after you sell it to her? How much are you going to be making anyway?"

He told her. "It's not the money." She said it sure as shit would be if it was hers. "I don't want to sell. Don't you women understand? This has been my company since I started out buying and selling before you were born."

"You're really stuck on age differences, aren't you? Whatever. Mr. Holland, how about she leaves the music player to you to run, and she takes the rest of the company from you to make it work?" He looked at Raven, and she did as well. "It's the only holdup, right? This dumbass idea he has that this thing will be a moneymaker?"

"Yes. It's the only sticking point we've run into. It's not ever going to show a profit. Not in this century or the ones to come." She turned back to Mr. Holland, but Raven spoke again. "If he takes this deal, where he runs the music part, it will be up to him to pay their payroll and buy materials for the part I'm not taking to work. I'm not going to be responsible for a product I won't own."

"You down with that, Mr. Holland?' He said he most certainly was not. How was he supposed to pay everyone if she took the profit-making part of his business? "I don't know. But you really should think about what you said. The music thing isn't making any money. But hey, that's not up to me. Okay, then I'll talk to Raven, and I'll convince her to walk away."

"Good. The sooner you're gone, the better things will be for me." Penny started away, Raven glaring at her from the table where she and her grandmother were sitting when she turned back to Mr. Holland. "I'm not going to change my mind. What is it now?"

"Call your wife, Mr. Holland." He asked her why. "You tell her you're going to receive seventy million dollars today for your entire company, and you get to walk away. Or you can tell her that you're not going to be able to go on vacation next year or whenever, no more trips overseas, because you're now stuck with a dying company, one that you've not been able to show a profit for in more time than I've been alive. See how I worked that in there? I can see that you enjoy traveling by the pictures on the wall. You tell her that you're going to make considerably less than the seventy million — nothing, as a matter of fact — that was offered because of the thing she wanted you to sell. Not only that, but you also have no capital, no payroll money, nor do you have your pension. Because if Raven and her grandma walk away from this, which is what I'm going to suggest they do, then you're going to prison. Not paying people for the work they're doing for you is a thing that will land you in prison faster than it would if you murdered someone."

"You're blackmailing me. Is that how you do business, young lady? I won't have it." She asked him again to call his wife. "I will, but I know what she's going to say. She's going to tell me to stick to my guns, and we'll make it work out some way or another."

While he called his wife, putting it on speakerphone for all to hear her turn down the money too, Raven smiled at her. "You make this work, and I will give you a bonus so large that you'll never be able to spend it all."

"I don't care about that. I'm here to hurry this meeting along so I can beat the shit out of you." Holly laughed as she sat down at the table again. "What the hell gave you the right to buy me all that crap without asking?"

"Would you have allowed me to do it if I had asked?" She said no. That she was standing on her own two feet. "You mean like Mr. Holland here is? I bought it because I see something in this that you might not just yet. You're selling all over the world, making a good but not fantastic profit, but you could be doing much better. You're very talented, Penny."

"I'm happy with making what I am." Raven just stared at her. "All right. I have wanted to branch out for some years now. But I don't have the start-up."

"You do now."

They both turned to the phone when Mrs. Holland answered. Penny hoped she didn't just fuck things up for Raven because she'd been pissed. Mr. Holland explained in great detail what was going on with his business.

"So, let me see if I have this right, all right, Herby?" He told her she was on speakerphone. "Good. When you hang up from this call, I hope you realize how smart you were for calling me. I love that you still think of me as a partner in our business deals as much as we are in life. I know this company is all yours, but if you walk away from the deal that makes us seventy million dollars, I will never speak to you again. We're not getting any younger, Herby. We don't have a lot of debt right now, and that feels good. But we could be doing so much more, don't you think? We could help our children buy new homes. Help our grandchildren with college. Go on those trips like we used to before the company took over your life. How many times have I told you I just want you home every night? More than I can count. Herby, you'd be a fool if you didn't take this deal from Mrs. Bishop. And I know for a fact that I didn't fall in love with a fool." He told her how the player he was working on would be finished. "It's just one item, Herby. A single thing that I happened to mention I missed. I've seen the paperwork. I know it's pulling down the entire company. Sell it before it's taken from you. Or worse yet, all this takes you away from me. Please. I want to see the world with you, right by my side."

Half an hour later, the deal was finished. Not only did Raven pay off the payroll before leaving, but Mr. Holland had his money in the bank. Holly also paid for tickets for the couple to take a long cruise, her treat. Raven told Penny that she was coming to dinner with her and Grandma.

"I have to get back there and figure out what the hell you've gotten me into." Raven just moved her along until she found herself sitting in a restaurant with a glass of water in front of her. "You really do think you're right about everything, don't you?"

"Yes. Most of the time, I am. I was, however, wrong about you." Penny asked her about what. "You didn't just close that deal for us, Penny, but you were also able to let that man save face when he thought for sure he was going to upset his wife. Without you, everyone would have been out of work in the morning. I would have shut the place down, then bought it from the bank for nearly nothing."

"Then why the hell were you working so hard at making him let you buy him out?" Holly answered this time. "All right, I can see that. You wanted it to be something that wouldn't piss off everyone that worked there. You had it in the bag, Raven. Surely you know that."

"No, I didn't. And as much as I'd like to have a good working relationship with people that will soon be working for me, had I had to take it from him, they would have been out of work as well. It would have bothered the couple for a long time. This way, they made a good decision together. There would have been tension that didn't need to be there, as well as a lot of disgruntled employees. That does not make for a happy work environment for anyone." Penny was embarrassed at the praise Raven and her grandmother were giving her. "You and I, with the help of my grandma here, can do a great deal together. Also, with Dwayne coming along with what he knows about land, there won't be anyone who can't be sold on something we want to help them with."

"All I did was make him realize it was a huge decision that he shouldn't be making on his own." Holly told her that was sometimes all it took. "I'll help you, but don't think I'm not still pissed off about your purchases."

"I tell you what, Penny. You pay me back in whatever product you think is worth it. I think you're underselling your items." She said she'd discovered that as well. "Good. That means you know you have to raise prices and do it soon. We're going to make a good team."

Penny didn't know about working as a team. However, she did find herself excited to go back to her barn and start working with the few colors she'd seen in the boxes. Wondering about how much it would cost if she were to get shelves put in the place, Penny wondered if that would be a good winter job for Wesley. He said he didn't have much to do during the downtimes.

~*~

James didn't particularly care for the way he was being treated around here. He thought that since his mother had been a long time residen:, he should be treated differently. Not that he was sure how that was supposed to work for him, but people were mostly snots.

He looked across the street to see his niece coming out of the bank that Emmie worked at. There was another snot, he thought as he crossed to see her. Penny had gotten very uppity of late. Then there was the whole thing about Mom's will. Where did her stuff go? Who owned the house and the car she'd had? The car was wrecked up, but he thought he could get some money for it.

"What do you want?" He told Penny that was no way to treat him. "Oh? And why is that? You just got out of jail. Do you want to go back? I will press charges, Uncle James. I've had about all of you that I can take."

"I want to know what the will said." She asked him why as she moved down the street at a fast clip. "Slow the fuck down. Are you off to the races or something? Where is the money from my mom's estate?"

She stopped so suddenly he nearly knocked her to the ground. "You do remember that she was my grandmother, too? That I am your niece?" He huffed at her. "Very mature. I'm busy. Tell me what it is you think I've done wrong to you. Then I'll tell you to fuck off again, and I can be left alone. Well?"

"What the hell is up your ass?" She stopped again, and he did knock her back this time. He'd meant to do it and was disappointed she didn't hit the ground. "Before I forget to remind you, I've set up a day that you and Dutch can get married. I paid for the license, so you'll have to pay me back for that."

"No." She took off at her fast pace again, and he was nearly out of breath when she had to stop at the crosswalk. James didn't think he'd ever catch up to her if she had been able to cross where she was standing. "Why are you still following me? I have a lot to do today, and none of it includes listening to you whine about whatever you're whining about."

"I should knock you on your fucking ass right now." She lifted her chin up but moved as he swung at her. She was laughing as she crossed the street. James was still standing on the other side when the Don't Walk sign blinked at him. He crossed anyway. It was funny to him to see cars scrambling around, trying not to hit him. "Keep it up, bitch, and you'll be laughing out your ass."

People stared at him as he stepped up on the other side of the street onto the sidewalk. James was trying to keep an eye on where Penny was headed next, but he lost her when she walked into a large group of people. Damn it all to fuck and back. He didn't get to tell her he was marrying Emmie soon too.

The more he thought about that, the better the idea was. The four of them could live in the house that had been his mom's. The women would go on working like they were now, and he and Dutch could make sure they never missed a sporting event. James figured that between the two of them, Penny and Emmie, there would always be something cooking in the kitchen, and the fridge would be full of beer. Just the way he liked it.

James didn't know shit about getting a license to get married. He'd only said that to his niece so she'd fork over some money to him. He had no idea why he thought that would work. Penny hadn't been all that generous in a long time. In fact, now that he thought about it, he didn't know if she even had a job.

"She has to have one." He crossed the street, no longer sure where she had gone. Thinking about her having to have a job got him sidetracked. Penny always seemed to have a couple of bucks on her. She also seemed to be gone a lot. Or was she only hiding from him? That was more than likely it. Penny had herself a hidey hole that he wasn't aware of. "Well, that's going to stop as soon as she's married to Dutch."

"You talking to yourself, young man?" He thought he knew the old man sitting on the bench, but he couldn't place him. "Who are you thinking is going to marry Dutch Donnelly? I know him, and I don't think there is a girl around that would willingly marry him. Either of you, for that matter."

"You keep your opinions to yourself, old man." The man laughed, and James told him that his niece was marrying Dutch. "And I'm going to be marrying Emmie. We'll have a nice home in my mom's old place and live like kings."

"I don't know how to break this to you, but your niece

is already set to get married." He asked him what he was talking about. "Yes. Penny is marrying my son, Wesley. They just got to get things all set up for first thing in the morning. It'll be the prettiest little wedding, I'm betting. I was just sitting here thinking about how lucky I am to have three of my sons getting married to the best little girls around."

"Why would my niece want to go and marry someone else when I told her she was marrying Dutch?" The old man, he knew he was a Bishop now, laughed at him. "What the hell do you think is so fucking funny? Now I have to go and kill her soon-to-be-dead husband so she and Dutch can get hitched. Why do women have to make things so complicated?"

"You think you're going to be able to take on my son? Well, you go ahead and give that a shot. Why don't you let me call him here for you? Might be some of the best entertainment going on these days." The man stood up and looked into the store he'd been sitting in front of. "Wesley? Come on out here, son. This man thinks he's gotta kill you for wanting to marry his niece when he had her all set up to marry that Donnelly boy."

There wasn't anyone in there. Bishop was lying to him to delay him. He didn't know why he'd care where he was going, or for that matter what he'd been up to, but it was a delay tactic all the same. Then his niece came out of the store. Just as he was drawing back to hit her in the face, he heard a small growl.

"You touch her, and I will tear your arm off and beat you to death with it." The threat—and there was no doubt that was what it was—was softly spoken and full of promise. Dropping his arm back to his side, James turned to see who the hell he thought he was. "My name is Wesley Bishop. Your niece, Penny, will become my wife as soon as I can arrange it. Now, I don't know where you get off thinking you would have any say whatsoever about who your niece marries, but she's a grown woman. She and I are to be wed, and if you have any idea to try anything towards her, I will kill you where you stand."

"She's supposed to marry Dutch. I'm going to marry Emmie, and we'll have a nice life." It sounded so whiney saying it like that that James felt his temper rise. "She has no right marrying someone I didn't approve of."

"Why? You're not even her father. Why would anyone care what your opinion is about this?" He said he was her caregiver. "At twenty-six, you think your niece is in need of a caregiver? I don't think you've taken a good look at Penny lately, James. She's an adult. I'm sure she votes and everything now."

"Fuck you." Wesley laughed as he put his arm around Penny. "Get your ass home and fix some dinner for your dad and me. I'm going to be finding out about my mom's will too. You know who got it all?"

"I did." He couldn't have heard her right. "I got it all. The house—which I'm going to be redoing and renting out—and the money she had in her account. There wasn't much, but it'll come in handy for the repairs that need to be done. Also, her insurance money. I didn't know she had any, but it was a nice chunk of cash."

"Give it to me." She didn't say anything, but she did laugh. "You heard me, Penny. Give me the money, and I won't say anything about you getting the house. But I do like the idea that you're going to fix it up. I'll live in it until you rent it. It would be better if you didn't try hard to rent it while I'm there. This is better."

He put out his hand, and she just looked at it before shaking her head. Wesley smiled at him like he knew some big secret. He more than likely did, but that didn't mean James was going to allow Penny to have the money. Being the oldest should have made him first in line for all his mom's things.

"When your mother was alive, James, what did you do to make her life better?" He asked Wesley what he was talking about. "You heard me. When she was alive, how many times did you go by the house and help her out with something? Mow the yard? Did you help her clean out the gutters? Anything? Or were you, just like you are now, there with your hand out waiting for her to turn something of value over to you?"

"What is your point?" Wesley just shrugged. "You ask that like you already know the answer. No, I didn't help her out. I have more important things to do than to sit around her house, waiting for her to find something for me to do. Yes, she did give me money when I asked, unlike my niece here. Hand it over, Penny. I'm not fucking with you right now."

"I told you what my plans are for the money. Not that you asked, but Grandpa Joe is living with us too. He's sad, but he's getting better every day." James said he'd take his house then. "I already own that, as of this morning. Well, Wesley and I own it. It's going to have to be torn down. Termites have gotten to the foundation."

"Are you going to give me anything, bitch? I'm broke, and it's all your fault." The need to hit her was great. But he knew as surely as he would draw back, her new husband would do just as he'd said and kill him. James tried being pitiful for her, so she'd help him. "You have to give me something. I'm down on my luck, Penny. I'm your uncle, for fuck's sake."

"You are. There is no doubt about that." She looked at Wesley, then back at him. "All right, I'll help you out. But just this one time. If I were you, I'd get a job. Nothing is free anymore, and you should have learned that a long time ago."

"Yeah, sure. Where is my money?" She said she'd never planned on giving him anything but advice. "That's it? You tell me to get a job, and that's supposed to help me? Christ, I should have left you with your fucking mother when I killed her."

"What did you just say?" James had to think about what he'd said and backed away from them. "You killed my mother? For what?"

"I don't know what you're talking about." He looked around for an easy escape to gather his thoughts. "I'm going to let you off this time, but you'd better be prepared to pay me some of the money I should have gotten in the first place."

He was nearing the police station when a group of cops came outside. Turning down the alley that ran the length of the station, he found himself a nice quiet place to hide out. She'd tricked him, he told himself. Tricked him into saying things he shouldn't have. Damn, damn, damn. James was beginning to really hate his niece.

Chapter 6

Wesley found Penny on the deck. She'd been absent for a while now, and he was relieved to have found her. He could have, he supposed, reached out to her, but he didn't know how she was feeling. Asking her if she was all right, his heart broke when she looked up at him. There were tears still falling, and he sat down in front of her and laid his head on her lap.

"If you want me to, I could go find him now and shake the answers out of him. I don't know how much he'll tell you, but it would be fun to do that." She put her hand on his head, and he turned enough to kiss it. "I'm so sorry he hurt you, Penny. I had no idea he'd done what he had."

"I think on some level, I knew he had." She lifted his head up and kissed him. "I thought for sure he was going to piss himself when you spoke to him. You were so calm, but I could tell you were angry."

"To be honest with you, I was trying not to allow you to kill him. I could see you were reaching for your gun." She laughed with him. "There are a couple of things I'd like to ask you. Nothing earth shattering, but just questions. Why is it that Tony never seems to come around? I mean, I don't know why, but I thought he and your uncle would be close."

"Dad hasn't really been around much even when he was in the same room with someone. He's forever quiet, unlike James." He thought it was because James never shut up and told her that. "There is that. He was forever trying to inject some of his stupidity into a conversation. I think Dad just got used to letting him have his way. I wonder if Dad had anything to do with Uncle James killing my mom."

"I don't know why I think this, but I don't think he did. I've seen your dad around town a couple of times lately, and he always seems to have his head down and moving quickly. I think you got that from him, racing from one place to the next." He stood up—the deck was cold on his ass—and picked her up out of the chair. Instead of sitting back down with her, he took her into the house and sat with her on the couch. "I was enjoying the fire in this room when I realized I'd not seen you since we got home today."

"It's nice, isn't it? To have a nice warm fire when it's so cold out. I bet this room will be the place we hang out the most when winter comes." He said he'd hang out with her anywhere. "You're just hoping to get laid again, that's all."

"Of course, I am. But I will admit, I'm sort of worn out." She just looked at him. "You're almost too much for me. I wonder if you're trying to kill me off or something."

"No. Not yet, at any rate." He remembered something and got up to find the envelope Raven had given him that morning. Handing it to her, he sat back down next to her as he explained. "Raven said this is the commission on sealing the deal the other day. She told me you did a fantastic job with it."

"I was pissed off that she had the nerve to buy me all this— Holy fuck, Wesley, this is for seven million dollars. What the hell is she doing giving me this much money?" Wesley said he'd not known about the amount, but he figured it would be high. "Why? Why on earth didn't you warn me?"

"Actually, I never thought about it. When she handed me the envelope, Chandler was there. He told me it would be a good amount as Raven and Holly paid him ten percent of each deal he helped close for them. I didn't know how much the original deal was for, but I thought you'd been told about it." Penny kept staring at the check. "Penny, are you hearing me?"

"Yes. This is a lot of money when all I really did was tell the man to call his wife." Wesley didn't know what to say to Penny about that, but he knew Raven had been glad she showed up. "I had to deposit my mom's insurance this morning. This is really going to make Emmie's day when I want to put this someplace safe."

When the front door was knocked on, he got up to let his brother in. He'd called him when they'd gotten home after talking to James, and Chandler said he'd help. He was happy to see he'd not only brought Sasha, but Pip, their daughter, as well. He took the baby and led them to the living room where he could sit and play with the baby while they spoke to Penny.

"Hey." Chandler had a way with words, he thought. But it was Sasha that spoke next. She wasn't one to beat around the bush.

"I don't know if you were told this or not, but Chandler and I can see ghosts." Penny looked at him, and he nodded. "Wesley asked us to come over here and see if you'd like to have some information about your mother. I told him I could do it easily, but not without your permission."

"You're not kidding, are you?" Penny got up and took Pip from him. When she sat down, she didn't look at them but the baby. He thought she was taking this much better than he'd expected. "I just found out today that James killed her. Will you know how he did it?"

"I will. You won't unless you wish to. I can talk to her for you. She can hear you, but I'm afraid she's been gone too long for me to be able to allow you to speak to each other. Chandler and I are getting used to this promotion, they called it, a little at a time. I will tell you, Penny, she'd not had a very easy life up until her death. I will also tell you that Tony isn't your father. I did find out that much."

"Is it James?" Sasha told her no, he wasn't either. "So,

my birth certificate is wrong. That neither of them are related to me."

"You *are* related to them. Wendy wasn't your grandmother, but your mother." Penny did look at Sasha then. "Wendy had you while her boys were in prison. She had sent you away to the Parker family to be raised. Hallie, the friend of Wendy's, was killed by James, and he brought the child, you, home for your brother. Tony and James aren't your uncle and dad—they're your brothers by birth. No one is sure why he knew to find you there. Only Wendy would be able to tell you that."

"Do you see her too?" Sasha nodded. "I don't know what to think about all this. I mean, I want to believe you, but it's so far out there I'm not sure what to think."

"I do understand that. Wendy refuses to use the glamor that is there for her. When she was in that accident, she told me, she'd just found out that James had killed Hallie. She was calling the police when she lost control of her car. The rest, you know."

Penny got up with Pip and paced the room. "Will she give me the answers I need if you ask her? Either of them?"

"Yes. Ghosts cannot lie to us. It hurts them when they try. I'm new to this stuff too. I mean, all of this is crazy nuts sometimes, but I do have Chandler to fall back on when it gets to be too much." Penny stopped pacing, and his heart broke for her tears. Wesley wanted to get up and make his family go away, but Penny needed answers. "What is it you want to know?"

"Did Hallie suffer?" Sasha glanced to her right and then told Penny she had. "I'm sorry. I know you said she can hear me, but could you tell her that I'm so very sorry for this?"

"She said to tell you it was never your fault. But she is glad to see you're happy now." Penny said she was. Very much so. Sasha laughed again. "She said to tell you she's glad you look nothing like your mother. Something I should explain. The two here cannot see or talk to each other. Unless they died together or they died at the exact same time, they can't see each other. It's only relatives that can have conversations on the other side. These two were friends at one time, but that isn't the same as being related."

"Will you ask Wendy why she had me sent away? I think I might know the answer to that, but I don't know for sure." Wesley looked at Penny while Sasha stared at whoever was talking to her. "I'm all right. I'm just trying to come to terms with this."

"It'll be all right, love. I just wanted to be informed when James or any of the others came around." She asked him if he thought Grandpa Joe knew. "I don't know. I would think he did. It's perhaps why he made it so you got everything in her will."

"Wendy said she'd been afraid that you'd be hurt by the boys. Mostly James. She said James has never been right in the head." Penny laughed, but it was forced. "Wendy said Grandpa Joe did know, and she's glad he did what he did. She might not have been happy about it at the time, but now she is. Also, she sent money each month to Hallie. You were with her for about a year, Wendy said."

"How did I end up being Tony's daughter on the paperwork?" Sasha locked at who he thought was Wendy. "Also, who's my father? Anyone that I might know?"

"There isn't a father's name on your birth certificate, just Wendy's as your mother. Tony only claimed you as his own verbally. I don't know why—he would have his own reasons, Wendy said. But she was happy for it. She believes Tony might well have known about you being Wendy's. When he mentioned it to James, saying he had a child out there someplace, James took it upon himself to go and get you. No one, not even Tony, she said, was aware that he'd done it until he showed up with you."

"So, Tony knew about me and told his brother, the psychopath, that he is my father. Why?" Sasha told her. "He found the birth records when looking for cash. Okay, that I can believe. He was forever going through drawers and cabinets looking for things to steal and pawn. So instead of asking his mother about them, Tony tells him that I'm his child. To what end, I'm wondering."

"She doesn't know." Nodding, Penny finally sat down and looked at Pip again. "Pip is going to be able to see ghosts too when she's a little older. It's the mark that the two of us bear that makes us what we are. I'm also to understand that when she stares at you like she is now, she sees a part of you that no one else can. I'm sorry I don't have better news for you, Penny."

"Are you kidding? You've given me a great deal. I didn't know any of this." Penny handed Wesley the baby. Then she got up to go to the door that led to the outdoors. He thought she was going to go out again, but all she did was stare out. "I have so many questions right now I can't think beyond I'm not who I thought I was."

Chandler cleared his throat. "I know where Hallie is buried. Her husband is also dead. They've been missing, and no one has been able to have closure since you were brought here. I'm going to have Sawyer make a few calls and have them found. They'll be able to tie James to their murders because of the stuff he left behind that he used to kill them both with." Penny asked if it would be enough. "Yes. More than enough. Allen, Hallie's husband, has more wounds than Hallie does. The things James used to kill them both are with Allen's body."

"That's enough on that, all right?" Chandler nodded at Penny and looked at Wesley and said he was sorry. Penny told him it was fine, really. "I have to tell you guys, I don't know whether to thank you for this or run screaming from the room. I believe you, but it's nothing I ever thought of. Not just that you can see ghosts, but that I'm not the person I thought I was."

"No. But I don't think for a minute that this will change you in any way. Just because you're not his child doesn't mean you're anything like either of them. You are who you are because of how you were raised." Penny thanked him. "I love you, Penny. With all my heart. And getting married to you only makes me want to love you more."

~*~

Butch was waiting outside the store when he heard someone talking as they came up behind him. He had to stare at the two women for a while before he realized it was his sister and Penny. Christ, whatever they were doing to themselves nowadays, it sure had prettied them up. When they moved by him, not acknowledging him at all, he reached out to grab Emmie and found himself slammed up against the building behind him.

"What the fuck, Emmie? Are you trying to piss me off? Let me go, and I'll only hit you a couple of times." She asked him why that would make her want to release him. "What? Just let me go, will you?"

She didn't release him. However, he stiffened when he felt the dangerous part of a gun poking him in the back. Butch just knew it was Penny that was the one carrying the gun. She was forever pulling that sucker out when there wasn't any reason for it.

When he was flipped around, no other word for it, he looked at his sister when she put a gun into his forehead. It startled him, even more, to know she had figured out to start carrying a gun too. Mother fucking balls, where were all these people getting guns from? He asked her what she thought she was doing.

"Keeping you from touching me. Making sure you know that if you do happen to touch me again, by just a hug or a fist, I'm going to shoot you. I don't care enough about you anymore, Butch, to be concerned about whether you live or die." He told her she was a cold bitch. "Perhaps. But I'll tell you this. It's much easier than it used to be to think about you being dead."

"I just don't know who you are anymore. Nope. Also, I don't care about all this change shit going on. You're a hard woman. What you think is going to happen when you marry James?" She said she wasn't marrying James. "Yes, huh. You're going to marry James, and Dutch is going to marry Penny. You'll live in that old house of Wendy's and have the best life ever. They've even decided you two can keep your jobs so they won't have to work."

"Well, isn't that nice of them." Butch didn't think she was being nice when she said that to him, but he didn't push his luck. Having her agree with him about them marrying up, he didn't care what else she said. "I'm not marrying anyone, you fucking idiot. I would like to have a nice husband that doesn't think his wife should do all the housework, cooking, and cleaning while still holding down a job."

"Why not? James is a good guy. He's been around the block a time or two in prison, but that ain't no different than me. You and Penny will be happy as fuck. And mentioning that, you'd be fucked nightly too. Ain't that worth the price of bread in China?" She told him it was price of tea in China. "I don't like tea. Why would I care about the—?"

"Listen, you uneducated potato head. I'm not marrying anyone you pick out for me. Neither is Penny. She's marrying a man of worth, and they'll have children no one has to worry about robbing a bank or anything like you've done. No. We're not marrying the likes of either Dutch or James." He told her she wasn't being fair. "Fair about what? Me getting married so I can be beaten all the time? You can bet your last buck I'm not going to do anything you think I should be doing."

"Why are you always so bitchy?" Penny laughed, and Emmie did too. It was mean laughter too. Not at all like they thought anything was funny. Women were so strange. "Penny, I'm going to tell your daddy on you. Seen if I don't."

"Good luck with that. He's been dead since James and Tony went to prison all those years ago." Butch was confused. He normally was, but right now, he didn't know what the hell she was talking about. Tony was dead? No way. "You're just as stupid as the rest of them, aren't you, Butch? I'm wondering if your parents realized that the two of you were going to be trouble from the second you took your first breath. I have a feeling had they known, they'd have put you up for adoption right away."

"Now that's just mean. We're all right people. We're no different than anyone else around here. Why, just the other day, I was telling my brother that I've been out of jail for nearly a month now without no one catching me. I think that's a world record for me." She just shook her head. "I bet that guy I heard you were marrying up with can't say that."

"You're absolutely right about that. He's never been to prison. Or jail for that matter. What do you know, you hold that record compared to a nice family." He wasn't sure, but Butch thought she was jesting him. But he did agree with her. "It's not a contest, Butch. Being out of jail for nearly a month isn't all that wonderful of a thing to be proud of."

"Why not?" She told him never mind. "You brought it up. Tell me what you're meaning. I'm right proud of not being caught at the shit I've been up to. You know I ain't been sitting around with my thumbs up my ass. I've been busy around town."

"Why don't you get yourself a job?" That actually made him gag. Nearly ready to puke on her shoes, he had to turn away and lean his head against the wall. "Are you seriously sick right now because I suggested you get a job? Christ, no wonder you're still single with no prospects of getting a better life."

"Oh, that wasn't nice, Penny. Not at all. You know I'm allergic to real work. Oh, I have to go and lay down. Wait until I tell my brother what you did to me." He stood there for a second longer, thinking about her nasty suggestion. When it hit his belly, he did puke up his lunch in the corner by the building.

Butch had a terrible headache when he stood up again, just at the thought of having to get to some place on time and to wear a uniform. Thinking about something else so as not to upset his belly again, he staggered home. That wasn't nice of Penny. Not at all. He had a good mind to tell her uncle about it. Or even her daddy. But then Tony didn't seem to care at all what his daughter was up to.

Walking home, he saw that people were out fixing up their shops. It took him a few minutes to realize it was getting close to Thanksgiving. His belly rumbled, this time in anticipation for a plate full of mashed up potatoes and some gravy. Oh boy, he thought, pie too. His favorite was cherry. His momma used to make the best cherry pie in the world.

Butch was going to have to talk to Dutch about their holiday with Penny. For some reason, he didn't think she'd be making them stuff to eat because he wanted her to. Emmie wouldn't do it either. She was forever telling them that if they wanted a home cooked meal to get in the kitchen and make it.

"Ain't my job, damn it."

His belly was empty now that he'd been sick, and he was suddenly starving for a thick slice of turkey with all the trimmings. When he saw a poster in front of the old people's home he stopped to make it out.

The pictures on it helped him some. Neither Butch nor Dutch could read all that well. Emmie could. When she lived at home with them, she'd read the newspaper and not tell them anything that was in it. She would, however, tell them when their names came up in an article. Then she'd go on about how they were still alive, as they'd not made it to the obit page yet. Emmie had always been mean to him and Dutch.

The turkey was one of them cartoon ones where it was dancing around the poster. Somebody had cut out a bowl of mashed taters as well as a boat of gravy. Green bean casserole wasn't anything he cared for, but he'd eat it in a pinch. He was getting to the numbers when someone came up behind him, their tall shadow blocking out the sun he'd been using to read.

"It says if you happen to have five bucks on you you can have a plate of Thanksgiving dinner." He turned enough to see it was one of them Bishops. He was just hungry enough to ask him to read it all to him. "It gives you the date, which was yesterday, as a matter of fact. So, I guess you're out of luck in having a meal at the church."

"Well that sucks. I never seen this until today." The man started to walk on, and he realized he was dressed in a pair of khakis like them army men wore. "You related to that one that thinks he's going to marry Penny? You tell him he'd better be backing off. My brother has dips on her."

"Dips? It's dibs, you moron. You know she's a beautiful woman, don't you? Not some spinach dip that you stick crackers in." He told the man it was a figure of speech. "That doesn't make it any less offensive. If she were here right now, I'm sure Penny would knock your head off. I would if I weren't in such a hurry. Stay away from her and

Emmie, or so help me, I'll make your life until now seem like a picnic."

Again, he didn't know what the man was talking about. He thought about the dips thing he'd said. All his life, Butch had thought it was silly that people would say they had dips on things. Now he knew why he'd never understood it. It wasn't right. Butch was going to tell his brother about that too when he heard him say it again. It's dibs, not dips.

Walking home, all he could think about was how empty his belly was. He knew for a fact that there wasn't any food in his place. The last time he'd been able to swipe something from the store had been a while ago. Now they had cameras all over the place. It was getting to the point where a man couldn't take a quick piss at the back of the bar without someone getting on him about it.

Butch realized he'd missed his house and had to turn back to go home. As he got to the end of the street, he realized he'd missed it again. It wasn't until he was standing in front of his old mailbox that he realized his house was gone. He'd seen the construction stuff yesterday that was just across the street, but he never would have thought of them taking his house.

It wasn't really a house. It was one of them storage sheds he'd gotten out of the dumpster about five years ago. It had a holey roof, sure, but he'd been able to fix that up with some tarps he'd found. It had power, thanks to the house beside his. Also cable. Not that he had a working television set, but he could have cable if he wanted.

He found what was left of his home in the big dumpster that wasn't there yesterday. Butch saw his plate that had gotten all busted up. There were his shoes. They pinched like the dickens, but he could wear them still. All his worldly goods were just picked up by some big moving thing and crushed up into a pile like nothing.

"Hey, you that man that was living back there?" He didn't know the man that was yelling at him from the house he'd been living behind. "You've been freeloading long enough. I told you a month ago to remove yourself and that eyesore, but you ignored me. I called the police, and they said that since I didn't want it there I'd have to have it taken down on my own. I did warn you."

"I wasn't bothering you none." The man told him he was stealing his electric and cable. Not to mention, it smelled back there. "Well, I ain't got no bathroom so I was using the outside. I want you to put that all back now. You had no right to take a man's home."

"I had every right. I didn't allow you to live there and I evicted you." He laughed and Butch asked him what was so funny. "You. Thinking that I'd put that mess back there and let you continue living there. Christ, you're as dumb as a post. Stay off my property or I'll get you for trespassing."

He started for the man, but the police pulled into his drive before he got anymore than a couple of steps. Taking off at a run—well, a sort of fast walk—he was headed back to town when he realized he didn't have a place to sleep tonight. And it getting cold and all. People were just mean, he thought to himself. Just as mean as a rattlesnake.

Dutch was just coming down the sidewalk on the other side of the street when Butch yelled for him. Dutch told him how he'd gotten out. "Who would have thought that someone forgetting to check a box that said he'd been read his rights would have been his ticket. His get outta jail card, like in that game." Dutch told Butch he thought he'd be able to lay low, at least until the marrying was done up right. He said he was going to have to stay with him tonight on account of him needing an address. Butch told him about his home.

"Are you kidding me right now? They actually tore down your house? What sort of people live in this town when a decent person can't even have a house of his own?" Dutch shook his head. "Well, I guess we'll have to go and see if James can put us up. This world ain't nothing but filled with sorry asses. I can't believe they tore your house down. That's wrong."

Butch decided not to tell his brother that James didn't have a house either. That someone had tossed him out a few days ago when he'd been in jail—for not paying rent or something like that. Well, they'd have to all bunk at Wendy's old place, he supposed. That was all they could do under the circumstances.

He didn't know where they were going to bed down, but he did keep his eye out for an empty store front or something. Anything to get in out of the cold. Just as they figured out that James was homeless too, it started to snow. Nothing was going right for them, it seemed. Not a durn thing.

Chapter 7

Wesley was headed out to the barn when he felt someone was near. Stopping on the little path he'd had made for just this, he turned and saw a figure coming out of the stand of trees. His first thought was that it was James standing there, holding a gun. Shifting to his tiger, he felt his cat's anger. Wesley snarled at the other man, swiping his claws at him to give him a warning. The gun dropped, as did the man when he started speaking.

"I'm Tony. I swear, I'm Tony. Don't hurt me." Wesley moved slowly toward Tony but didn't touch him. As Wesley leaned into his shoulder, the man whimpered just as Wesley realized it wasn't James, but indeed Tony. "I'm not here to hurt anyone. I promise. I just want to speak to you."

Wesley knew that Penny was close. He reached out to her to ask her to come to him. *Your dad — I mean, Tony is here. I've shifted because I didn't realize it was him, and now I can't speak to him to let him know I have to go in and get dressed. Unless he wants to speak to me while I'm naked. Which, I don't think he would.*

I'm doubting that as well. She came around the side of the house, laughing and spoke to Tony. "He is going to run into the house to redress. Why are you here this early in the morning, Tony? Something going on?"

Wesley heard him tell Penny the same thing he'd told him that he wanted to speak to him. Grabbing the first thing he touched from the clean laundry, he pulled on a pair of jeans and a T-shirt as he looked around for a pair of shoes. Damn it all to hell and back, he'd torn them to shreds when he'd shifted. And that was his favorite pair. Leaning out the back door, he asked Penny if they could come into the house. He had to find some shoes.

Both of them entered the house just as he found a pair of clean socks. He usually didn't wear socks around the house, but the new floor was wooden, and it was colder than the carpet that had been in the other house. But he loved the easy clean up of the floors here.

When Tony said they could talk in here, he sat down at the dining room table with him as Penny made them all some tea.

"I'm sorry I startled you." Wesley laid the gun that Penny had given him on the table. "Why are you armed, Tony, if you only came here to talk? I'm not a man to take chances. I probably would have attacked you anyway had

I seen the gun before I saw you."

"I don't blame you." He didn't say anything else while Penny was out of the room. Tony looked around. He smiled at some of the paintings on the wall and even got up to look out the double doors that led out onto the deck surrounding this end of the house. When Penny arrived, he sat down. "I'm not Tony. I'm Randal. I live here with Tony. We all do."

Neither he nor Penny said anything. Tony or Randal just sat there, sipping his tea. When he picked up one of the cookies on the little plate, he ate it daintily and was careful of not getting crumbs on the table. It was Penny who spoke first.

"I'm sorry. I heard what you said, but I don't understand. You've been called Tony all my life." He said the man she knew as Tony was there as well, but he was Randal. "You're telling me that you've been lying about your name all this time?"

"I think he's telling you he is only one of multiple personalities." Mr. Joe came in and sat down with them as he continued. "I wasn't eavesdropping, but I did hear what he said and wanted to come and find out myself. However, I believe I've noticed some of the people that Tony is. I don't know really how to explain this, but I think what Randal here is trying to tell you is that the man we all knew as Tony Harold isn't the only person in there with him."

"That's right. Tony is our host, I guess you could

call him. Over the years of growing up, there have been others that have manifested here. When we decided it was time, one of us came to explain this to your husband, it was thought I could be the calmest about it." Randal took Penny's hand in his, and Wesley wasn't surprised to see her jerk it away. "I'm sorry, Penny. Tony said to tell you, however, that he has loved you since the day you were brought to him. I'm sure you've found out that he's not your biological father. But he did love you as his child. He has—we all have tried to protect you as best we could."

"I don't understand." Penny looked at Mr. Joe and him. "I don't know what is going on here. What do you mean he has different personalities? That's not possible. I mean, they do it on movies all the time for the thrill factor, but not in real life."

"You've noticed it too, Penny." She shook her head as she looked at the man she'd only known as Dad. "You have. And recently. When you were in the grocery store several weeks ago, James came at you. He was ready to hurt you. But Joey, another person here, he was there for you and ran him off. Do you remember what you said to him?"

"I said thank you, whoever you are. I was joking." Randal just watched her. "Another time you came to my aid, I had fallen down outside the shed, and you were there with the first aid kit. You said something to me. You said that...you said you told Tony this was going to happen if that shed wasn't taken down. I didn't know what to think, so I just didn't. Think about it, I mean."

"Correct. If you were to think about it, you'd remember other things too. Other times one of us tried to tell you that you were never alone. That one of us — as I said, all of us — were there for you." Penny got up and left the room. Randal looked at Wesley. "I need to speak to you about a few things. There are things you must know in order to make sure James is put away. We should be as well. Not for any crimes. I assure you, Wesley, that none of us have harmed people or committed any crimes that should put us in prison. But we should be put away. Before we harm our host."

"That's why you have the gun." Randal looked at the gun and then nodded at him. "Why? What's going on that any of you feel you should end his life? If you've caused no trouble, what is the reason you have for wanting this?"

"We're too much for him." Wesley didn't know what that meant, but Penny came back then with several envelopes. Spreading the contents of one of them onto the table, it was Mr. Joe that started stacking them in some kind of order. "You knew even when you were in school. Didn't you? I saw the looks on your face when I was the only one around when you needed something. We've all noticed it from time to time."

"The signatures are different on my report cards I brought home. See? I got into trouble once in school because they said I was faking my father's signature. Then I went to live with my grandparents, and it wasn't brought up again." Mr. Joe said that was the reason she'd come to live with them. "You knew? You knew he wasn't the same man?"

"No. I wasn't sure. Your grandma did. She said there was something wrong with Tony. Nothing really wrong, she'd tell me, but there was trouble with him. I don't rightly think she understood it back then. I know I didn't. But when Tony would come around, I started noticing little things about him that I might not have if she'd not mentioned it." He pointed to one of the signatures on a report card. "If I'm not mistaken, I'm thinking one of you is a lefty."

Randal laughed and said that two of them were. He was the one that had signed that day. Penny sat there, not saying anything as Randal explained why he had come today. Wesley was more worried about Penny than he was anything the other man was saying until he mentioned James again. This time he did listen up.

"What do you mean he's the one that killed his mother? I thought it was ruled an accident. That she'd been on her cell phone when the accident occurred." Randal said she had been. "Then how is that his fault?"

"If the police would have checked who she was talking to prior to the accident, they would have known she was speaking to James, and that he was only a mile ahead of her when their call was cut off. James is the one that plowed into his mother's car. The dead man beside him was thrown from the truck just the way he'd planned it. None of us are sure what would have happened if he would have been killed or even hurt more than he was. But as I said, he had planned it well, and the other man was blamed for driving." Penny got up to pace, but she didn't speak as Randal continued. "We have proof enough for you to go to the police. The ball bat that he murdered the driver with is in the basement of his mother's home. I've checked — it's not been disturbed with all the remodeling."

Randal told him where it was. Wesley asked if he could call his brother, Sawyer, a retired cop to go and get it. He thought that was an excellent idea. Instead of reaching out to him, Wesley pulled out his cell phone and called his brother. He was laughing when he answered the phone.

"You're not going to believe this, Wesley, but I've been— What's happened? I can feel you're—well, I can't tell what it is I'm feeling from you, but tell me." He told him everything after putting it on speakerphone so that he could understand the strangeness of how he was feeling right now. "You're saying that Tony Harold has multiple personalities and that he's helping you put his brother away? I don't mean to sound like I'm bragging or anything, but I had a feeling there was more to Tony than him just being Penny's father. I'm on my way over if that's all right."

"Yes. I'd like you to be here when I tell them the rest of what I have to say." Randal sounded different now that Wesley believed he was a different person than Tony. "You're understanding now, aren't you, Wesley?"

"I wouldn't say that I understand, no. But I can see differences I didn't before. Out in the yard, you weren't Tony. I don't know why, but I think my cat noticed that quicker than I did." He said his cat was attuned to things like that. "I guess so. What I don't understand is why are you just now coming here with this information? I mean, you could have had him arrested long ago."

"How long do you think he'd have stayed in jail had it come out that his brother had multiple personalities, and that he'd been the one who had told on him? I had to wait on things to go in a certain way. Mostly that Penny would be safe." Wesley asked him if he thought she was safe from James. "Oh, yes. She has been since the moment you found her. There were other things that needed to be in line. The most important thing was that the house, thankfully, someday soon would be renovated, and they'd find the bat. There are other items that can be found that will link him to murders. I believe your brother is looking into two such murders now."

"Yes, the murder of Penny's biological parents. I didn't know there was any doubt that the accident that killed your mother was anything but an accident." Entering the room as he spoke, Sawyer shook hands with Randal, and Wesley was glad when Raven left the room with Penny. She was looking stressed. "I have to ask this. Not just so that I know, but also for my peace of mind. Is this some sort of revenge tell-all? In a way that shifts all the blame from you to your brother? It's my job to warn you that when the evidence comes out, I won't hesitate a moment to come after you if this is going to come back and bite someone in the ass."

"You always were a good cop. I've known that since the beginning." Something was different again. This person spoke in an older, much more gravelly voice. Mr. Joe noticed it as well and sat up straighter in the chair as if he knew this one. "Hello, Joe. It's been a long time, hasn't it? My name is Presley."

Mr. Joe just shook his head as he began to talk. "We used to pretend, you and I. Tony, he'd come to see me, and we'd talk for hours on end. But it was you, wasn't it? I did wonder at times how the boy was able to keep in character so well." Mr. Joe started sobbing. "You saved me a million times. You know that, don't you? You'd come around as Tony and get me to talking so I'd not do anything stupid with my wife gone. The things you knew, it astonished me that you could relate to me so well."

"You saved us as well. There were times when we'd go there just to be with someone that cared. We all know Wendy was your daughter, but she wasn't the motherly sort. As we got older, you would even hug us like we were something you treasured more than you did anything in this world." Mr. Joe said they were. They were his grandchildren, even the others like him with Tony. "Yes. We knew you'd say that. To count us in as family too. It was why we were able to go through life with James around and not be a part of what he has been doing."

It took the people that had knowledge of James almost three hours to get all the information to Sawyer. Different people within Tony all had a story or incident to tell. A couple of times, Sawyer had to get up and walk around, he told them. Having to solve this many cases done by one man was almost too much for him to imagine. What Wesley noticed and was so very proud of his brother for, he never once asked if the other personalities had helped James with these crimes. Nor did he seem disbelieving of what they were saying to him.

As it turned out, there were enough things that involved Dutch and Butch, too, that would hopefully put them away for a long time. He hoped so. The simple fact that the idiots still thought Penny and Emmie were to marry someone that they wanted was enough to make his belly churn up.

~*~

Penny was enjoying working in her new area. It had taken a longer than she'd anticipated to get things organized, but now that it was, for the most part anyway, she was working again. As she stood there looking over the design she wanted to work on next, she looked up when Wesley came into her shop.

"If you don't mind, I'd rather not talk about what went on in the house this morning. Not for a while yet." He said Raven had told him that when she and Sawyer left. "She's a wonderful and scary person, isn't she?"

"Yes. But why are you saying that?" Penny told him

what they'd been doing out here. "Ah. So, she finally convinced you to let her put your product online to a larger demographic, did she?"

"More like she bullied me into it. But she was right. She showed me the numbers of one of the companies that she owns that did it, and they tripled their profits by seventy percent. I told her I wanted to ease into this. I think what I said went into one ear and out the other. She's going to overwhelm me, I just know it."

"You don't look stressed right now. Or is that because you aren't thinking about what this might mean for you?" She said she was only thinking about one thing at a time. "Good idea. I do that too. When I'm working in the spring, I get that way. Overwhelmed by how much I want to plant and get ready for the season. So, I make me a list and then check the things off one at a time. It's what I do to keep me focused."

"I do that too." She pointed to the wallboard that had been put up for her over the last few days. "I know I could write on it then erase things off as I do them. But I love being able to tear up a little note that I've hung there. It's sort of like a feeling of accomplishment for me."

Wesley told her he could understand that completely. As he wandered around the room, she worked out the pattern she wanted in the placemats she planned to make. It wasn't an order, but something she wanted to do for their own house. Raven told her that she needed to do that more often. Instead of taking orders, she should put out a few items that were one of a kind.

"Will that work?" Raven told her that people who already followed her would be buying that kind of stuff up because it was a one of a kind. "I have always wanted to be able to just come out here and do my own thing. Well, not here, but when I was working before. It was sort of boring to make sure I got the same pattern in everything I did."

"Then do it." Penny thought about how neither of them mentioned what was going on in the house. "You're going to be all right with this. Growing into a larger art community will open doors for you all over the place. You know that, don't you?"

Penny said she thought so as well.

"When you're out here, what is it you miss the most?" She had completely forgotten Wesley was with her. She asked him what he meant. "You're going to be out here on a schedule now, you told me that. What is it that you'd like to have out here that would make working a schedule easier? I see you have a fridge. That's good. You also have a computer, as well as a printer. I imagine that saves you from going into the house for orders. What is it you want? Not for the business, but for you. Your own little addition to this place."

"I don't know." She looked around the large area and smiled at him. "Is this your way of getting out of putting shelves up for me? I have to tell you, I never will mention anything to Raven again. She's one to take over, isn't she?"

"She is at that. And while I can plant a garden without

any issues, building something, even as easy as it sounds to put up shelves, is not something I think I can do. So, I hired some people from the local pack to come and do it. They could use the income as well." Penny told him that was a wonderful idea. "Thank you. For as much as I'd like to take credit for it, it was Gunner's idea. He remembered the shelf I made for Mom when I was in grade school. I doubt I'll ever live that down."

"What happened to it?" She started laughing as he explained. "Wesley, even I know that one nail wouldn't hold up much on a shelf. I'm glad you've learned something from that. My shelves need to be sturdy. Thanks to Raven."

"As you said, she's pushy." She watched as he seemed to glide around the room. He asked her about colors and the material she used for different things. "This is nice here. I see where you're going with this now. You're wanting to stack them up by colors. That's a wonderful idea."

"I've never had to do that before." He turned and looked at her as she moved toward where he was. "Usually, I just go with the same colors, so it wasn't that big of a deal. But now, I have seventeen shades of green that I never used before. Also, there are different weights to some. For heavier or lighter usage."

Pulling one of the colors off the table where she'd put some of the material, she showed him the variations of the cloth. Penny realized he wasn't paying attention and looked at him, asking him why he was so interested in her work.

"I'm interested in anything you might be doing out here. However, the reason I came out here is because I thought I could perhaps help you break in a table or two. You don't have any space open that I can use." He pouted at her, and Penny couldn't help but laugh. "Laughing at a man who just had all his hopes dashed is sort of mean."

"Actually, I was thinking about how I've not had a lot to do with your cat. I mean, I have seen him, but it's always been in a position that there were other people around." He asked her if she wanted to have some fun with him. "In fun, do you mean having sex with me? Because that is a hard no."

"No, not that at all. Sheesh, woman. I only meant that he could chase you through the woods. Every time he catches you, you have to remove one article of clothing. Then when you're naked, I'll shift back and take you hard out in the open air." She asked him if he were so sure he could catch her. "Oh, a challenge, is it? Sure. What would you like to have of me should I concede that I can't find you?"

"An entire night of pampering and making love." He told her he'd do that for her anyway. "I meant you. I'd pamper you and make love with you all night. How's that sound?"

He kissed her then. She could feel his hunger, almost taste his need to take her. So, when he backed from her, she was slightly disappointed. Then he pulled off his shirt as he toed off his shoes.

"I will have to make sure I leave some clothing out here from now on." She nodded as she watched him strip down for her. "You keep looking at me like I'm a thick juicy steak, and we'll never make it outdoors."

"I can live with that." She pulled him to her, pressing her entire body to his as he did the same to her. It was earthshattering, his touch to her skin. "I can smell you, how wet you are for me. We're not going to make it, love."

He dropped to his knees and tore her pants from her. She was going to have to put clothing out here as well if he came out often. When he suckled her clit into his mouth, she held onto the table directly behind him. When her legs began to tremble, and her breaths were too much for her, she begged him to slow down. To give her a moment.

I don't think so. I don't think that's what you really want, either. Penny screamed when he bit down on her clit. Stars danced over her closed eyes. Her nerve endings were now awake, it felt like, and making her very aware of what Wesley was doing to her. *You taste of heaven and sweetness at the same time. I could do this all day long and never get enough of you.*

Penny was sure if he did try and do that for any longer than ten minutes, she'd be dead. As it was right now, she needed to lie down and hang onto something at the same time. Begging him again, she was ready to fall on her ass when he shifted his body around, helping her to the floor.

Come for me, Penny?

She couldn't help it. For as much as she wanted to

hold out on him, her body belonged to him and only him. Digging her fingers into anything she could touch, she screamed out her releases. Several times she had to inhale harshly as wave after wave of ecstasy cloaked her.

As he moved up her body when she begged him to stop, he nipped at her skin, her breast, and her navel as he journeyed to her mouth. He tasted of her juices. It was a heady feeling to know that he'd drank her down. Holding his head to her, she explored as much of his mouth as she could, tasting more and more of her as her tongue rolled throughout his mouth.

Wesley wrested with his pants to remove them. Finally, in the end, he just ripped them off. She could see his restraint, almost see his full cat as he snarled and growled. When he entered her, making her eyes roll to the back of her head, Penny screamed at the delicious pain that made them one.

He fucked her hard, taking her to heights she'd never been to before. Every time they made love, it was like it was all new to her, like having sex with a different person each and every time. Sometimes he was gentle; other times, he was consuming. But when he was like he was now, in control of both their bodies, it was all she could do to hang onto him. Much less keep up with him.

"Come for me, love. Now. Please come for me."

She came again, holding onto his shoulder, keeping her teeth in her mouth so she'd not bite him. But when he leaned into her throat, having him so close, she licked her tongue over his pounding pulse, hoping it would sedate her need to taste his flesh. It wasn't nearly enough.

She felt empowered when he bared his throat for her, like she knew whatever she was about to do would change things. Not just for her but for the two of them. Feeling her teeth by running her tongue over them, she first licked then bit down as hard as she could on the hottest part of his neck, directly over his beating pulse.

There was no sound for perhaps an hour, it felt like to her. It could only have been a few seconds, long enough for her body to go to its highest point of sensations to releasing it all from her mouth. She heard herself scream, felt the rawness of her throat as it escaped her. During it all, her mouth filled over and over with the most wonderful tasting elixir she'd ever experienced.

Dizzy with the sounds and colors that made themselves known to her, she let it ride over her as she swallowed again and again. Moving away from her bite, dropping her head down to the hard concrete, she watched in fascination as it sealed itself just before Wesley bit her.

Even with what she'd just experienced, she was still overwhelmed with these new feelings. She was being lifted up, tossed around, then held gently in his arms as she came again and again. When he drew deeply on her throat, every single cell in her body felt as if it exploded inside her. Then when he came, his cock stretching her beyond anything she'd ever felt before, Penny let go of her hold on her body and slipped over the edge of the cavern and let herself be blissfully taken under.

Not another sound came to her. Nothing impinged on her epic release. As she laid there, her heart full of love, Penny knew that on some level, she had achieved one of the greatest gifts ever given. She had become one with not just Wesley, but his large white tiger as well.

Chapter 8

Dressed from head to toe in black, Gunner stood on the rooftop and coiled up his rope for his descent to the window that he knew was the apartment where Jackson lived. It wasn't his real name. He'd figured that out a few days ago when he'd been searching for him. As soon as he had the rope just the length he wanted, he knotted it off around the air conditioner unit and was as ready as he'd ever been. Taking a deep breath in, he was ready to take the leap when someone screamed at him.

Don't do it! He nearly fell backward off the fucking building when he realized it had been Chandler. Asking him what the fuck he was doing, his brother asked him to give him a moment. He'd been awakened from a deep sleep. *Just don't do anything until I can wake up. Something is wrong.*

You don't even know where the fuck I am. What the hell

is wrong with you? Good Christ, you nearly made me fall. Chandler told him not only which building he was on, but also that his rope was a new one that he'd gotten at the hardware store six months ago. *What are you doing? Spying on me? What do you want?*

Ruby is here. He only knew one Ruby, and she was— *She's one of the three ghosts that follow you around all the time. I didn't mention them because they didn't seem to be harming you. But Ruby said you're not to engage with Swartz.*

How the—? She came to you to tell me not to go into the apartment? Why not? He coiled his rope up again and tied it back to his belt. Moving to a place where he could sit without being seen, he waited for his brother to tell him. *Chandler, if this is a joke, I'm not laughing.*

She said to tell you that not only is he waiting on you, but that Swartz, the real name of the man you know as Jackson, has four men in the place to kill you as soon as you enter. He asked him how she'd know. *How do they know anything, Gunner? They get around in places that none of us can. All right. Now, she's telling me to tell you to go to the other side of the building. There is a medium sized building there that you can hide behind. Also, she wants you to keep an eye on the western sky. There are drones out looking for you.*

Not taking any chances, he moved just where he'd been told. As soon as he was seated, his black clothing blending well with the dark shadows of the building, he saw the drone fly over where he'd been standing just a few minutes ago. He decided whatever was going on at

Chandler's home, he was going to listen.

Does she know how he knew I was coming here today? Gunner kept an eye out for another drone, as he could hear it coming. Once it buzzed by him, he laid down on the rooftop where he was and kept as still as he could. *What's the holdup?*

The holdup is you can either cut me some slack here, or you can very well get your ass shot off. I was dead asleep when she screamed for me to wake up. Scared the living shit out of me. I not only fell out of the fucking bed, but I hit my head on the bedside table. So, fuck off and let me listen to her. Gunner couldn't help it, he laughed. *Laugh it up, soldier boy. I'm doing the best I can here.*

Soldier boy? Like I've never heard that before. Gunner, for as scared as he'd been a few minutes ago, was enjoying this. He heard a shuffling sound nearby and pulled his gun to kill whoever was up there with him.

Don't shoot. They won't see you. Apparently, one of the older ghosts with you can use some kind of magic over you. Just don't move. The man did indeed come to stand within an inch of where he was lying. He even looked right at him. As he turned away, Gunner heard him give the all-clear to someone else that was with him. *She said to tell you there is a man with you, a ghost, that will take care that one of the two there with you is gone.*

Gunner heard the man scream as he fell off the roof. Not moving, Gunner did wonder how a dead person could do something like shoving a person off the roof. He didn't move. Whatever was going on around him, there was little he could do that wouldn't involve getting his ass shot up.

Okay, for now, you're safe, but stay right where you are. He told Chandler he wasn't moving. *The man, Swartz, is with four other men in the apartment you were going to enter. They're armed, but then I'm assuming you are as well. Gunner, I can move through the air in the other realm, and I'm going to go with Ruby to check some things out. I can't help you when I'm in that state. I don't know why; I'm just figuring this shit out a little at a time. But don't make me worry about you getting hurt. All right?*

I'm not moving. But if you come to see me in that ghost world or whatever the fuck it is, I'm going to leap off this building too. Just do whatever you need and don't come let me see you.

Chandler was laughing. Just as Gunner was going to join him, it cut off as if Chandler had been muted.

His brother was gone for what seemed like forever. Just as he was thinking he needed to check on him, just to make sure he was all right, Sasha spoke. Her calm voice made him think he might be all right.

Chandler might need you to do something for him. Well, not him, but the three women currently tied up in the apartment. He thinks their plan was for you to be found dead with them, and to be blamed for their murders. They're all alive, but not for long. They've been tied up for the last several days without any food or water. He asked Sasha if she knew why they thought this would work. *It's been done before, with this same group. They find an adversary, and they make sure the person is taken out in* such a way that not only do people love that he or she is dead, but they are hated too. *I don't know the reasons for that, but it's sort of their MO.*

So, I can go into the apartment now? She said he could, but he was going to go in through the front door. *Well, that sounds boring. But seriously, how am I going to be less shot up now that I'm going to be going in that way?*

They're not expecting you to be so boring, I guess. She laughed when he did. Gunner usually didn't have this much fun when he was out doing a job. *The drones have been taken care of. I'll tell you when this is over if you want to know how. You're to get up from where you are and go down the fire escape on the right side of the building on the front side.*

He moved just the way she'd told him to do. He didn't know how they were doing this, but he was happy with the help. Gunner would have been hurt. They all knew they were immortal; Sasha had explained that to all of them last month. However, his momma wouldn't be happy if he were to get hurt. She sort of liked him, he thought.

Halfway down the fire escape, he paused when Sasha told him to. Just as he did, he saw someone come out of the building and stand there smoking. When they were finished, they went in, and he moved on. This was fucking amazing, Gunner thought. It was like having eyes all over the place.

Okay. Now that you're at the bottom — please don't freak out — look at the window across the street. You should be able to see glimpses of Chandler. He started to tell her he wasn't dead, but he saw him. His brother was about three feet off the ground with big fucking wings flapping behind him. *I told him you'd not freak out.*

I don't usually freak out when working. I don't want to know how the fuck he's doing that. She said he didn't. *Now what?*

Follow Chandler. You might lose him while you're walking behind him. It's okay. Just wait where you saw him last, and he'll come back for you. It's hard for him to hold himself so that you can see him, so bear with him. Okay? He said he would. *All right. The door is unlocked, so go in. You don't need to help Chandler in.*

He waited until his brother entered before he did. It was habit. As he followed his brother up the stairs, he was careful to keep an eye on each level he had to go up. Gunner only lost his brother twice. Almost as soon as he realized he couldn't see him anymore, Chandler came back for him. It wasn't as if he was solid, but he wasn't clear either. Chandler's wings would blow over him if he got too close to him. That did freak him out a little. The scent that blew off his brother was floral like you'd smell in a funeral home. Gunner made sure he stayed back far enough after that.

All right. There are three doors in front of you. He told her he could see them. *Stand in front of the middle one. Now, I'm going to use a clock to help you with it. You're at six. There is a man at two and another man at seven, right inside the door you're standing in front of. Shoot the two o'clock first. He's pointed toward the door.*

Are you going to tell me when to go? Sasha asked him to wait just a moment. *You tell me, honey, and I'll do what you want. So far, this has been much better than me having to explain to Mom how I got my ass full of holes.*

Gunner, the man at two is talking, and I'm listening to him. She didn't speak for a few moments, and he was just fine with that. *All right, here is what's going on. There is trouble elsewhere. I've given Sawyer a heads up. But as soon as you're finished there, you go to him. The police know you're in this building and that you're helping your brother. Sawyer is hilarious when he's woken up from a deep sleep too.*

Gunner smiled. When she told him to go in, Gunner shot just where she told him to. The man at two o'clock was dead before he turned the gun to the second man and killed him as well. Sasha told him when the man was coming out of the kitchen and how high up to shoot, as well as the man that was coming out of the bathroom. Christ, he'd killed four men without any of them firing their own weapons.

Then he saw Swartz. Hitting the man in the face with his fist, Sasha warned him not to kill him. He wanted to, badly, but he didn't. As he was wrestling the man to the floor and holding him down, the door that he'd come through was filled with cops with their guns out and screaming at him to drop his weapon.

"I'm Navy SEAL Special Forces Major Gunner Bishop. I'm working with Sawyer Bishop." The cops seemed really jumpy to him, so he moved carefully and spoke calmly.

Just then, Chandler appeared to him and pointed to the room down the hall. "There are three women down the hall that are going to need medical attention now. If you'd call the team in, I can go and help my brother with the other issue."

It took them twenty minutes to release him. Even then, they didn't really want to let go of him in the event something else came up. When he left the building, the women were getting treated and the dead where being identified. Gunner got onto his bike and raced to the address that his brother, now back at home, had given him.

You didn't say retired. Gunner asked Chandler what he said. *When you told those men who you were, you never mentioned that you were retired. You're still working for the government, aren't you?*

Yes. When Chandler didn't say anything else, Gunner asked him what he was coming up on with Sawyer. *Am I just making an excuse, so I don't get caught up in what is going on at the other place?*

No. There is trouble in town. I didn't want Sasha to tell you before because I was afraid you'd hurry through what was going on there and get — Gunner said his name. *James has Penny hostage. Sawyer was on his way to you when Wesley called him. He'd been knocked unconscious, and when he woke up, Penny was gone. Mr. Joe thinks he shot James, but he's not sure.*

Does anyone know where he is? Chandler paused just enough that he had to pull over so he could listen. *I'm off the road now. Tell me what it is you're trying very hard not to tell me.*

Emmie was shot, and while expected to make it, she's in bad shape. Mr. Joe is with her. James shot her when he found her outside in the yard. Butch is dead as well. He was killed, from what it looks like, by Dutch when he found him in their mother's home. James and Dutch are holed up in the house that is being renovated next door to his mother's. The bat that James used to kill the driver of the semi that hit his mom was pulled out of there today. James knows it. Christ, Gunner thought, glad that no one had told him. *You're to go to Sawyer. He's in the front yard of the house, trying to get them to let Penny go. I'm to make sure you know this. I don't think that is what they expect you to do, however. Also, you're not to engage, but to report to Sawyer.*

Fuck that shit. Can you get me in there? He said he couldn't, but Sasha could. It took too much out of him. *All right. I'm about ten minutes away. I'll be at the back of the house. Ask her to meet me there. Where is Wesley?*

At the back of the house, waiting on you.

Gunner didn't know why he thought that was what he was going to be told, but he didn't expect anything less from Wesley. It was his mate, after all.

~*~

Wesley knew that going into the house would not only get him hurt but Penny as well. Also, he'd promised Sawyer he'd wait for Gunner to come. He'd also told him to not enter the building with his other brother, but that just wasn't happening. Wesley thought Sawyer figured that as well.

"You're not going to get yourself killed, are you?" He turned and looked at Gunner as he came across the yard. Grabbing his brother, he hugged him tightly, telling him he didn't want his wife hurt. "None of us do, Wesley. We'll get her out. You have to promise to listen to me, all right?"

"So long as you don't try and tell me not to go in, then I promise." Gunner told him he'd never do that to him. "Then I'll follow you to the letter. I swear it on my wife's heart."

Sasha had been talking to him the entire time he'd been there waiting on Gunner. She told him Penny was being her usual self. She was making sure both men knew they were going to die tonight, and she was pissed off that they'd hit Wesley.

You had better follow Gunner, or I'm going to have every ghost I know come after you. He promised her the same as he had Gunner. *Well, I can't ask for anything better than that. Just follow him closely, Wesley. Once she is out, we'll go into town and have a big breakfast that you can pay for.*

Anything you want.

Gunner handed him a gun, and he took it. Since Raven had been a part of their family, Wesley had thought it a good idea to know how to use a weapon. He could use one when he was out in the field, but this was killing a man. Could he do it? Only time would tell.

Without another word, the two of them went into the house. Twice Gunner told him to pause, and he did. So long as he didn't tell him to stay, he was going to get his wife out. Gunner stopped moving just as they were in the kitchen.

James is in the living room. I can take him if you think you can go into the basement and get Penny. He said he could. *No one seems to know where Dutch is, so watch your step. Don't do anything stupid.*

I'm going to get my wife.

Gunner stared at him. Wesley could tell that he wanted to say something, but all he did was nod toward the door that led down and move to the kitchen. Instead of going right down, Wesley laid the gun aside and shifted to his cat. He figured he had a better chance of not only finding Dutch but getting Penny out safely.

The stairs were tricky, as they were slick. Making his way down them, he took his time. His cat could sniff out Dutch better than he could as a man, so he didn't want to fuck that up. He knew Penny was alive, but he also knew she was hurt. The fucking bastard was going to pay for that.

He saw Penny lying on the floor. There was blood around her body, but he didn't know how badly she was hurt. However, to go to her now, he knew he could be walking into a trap. That Dutch was just waiting for him to go there so that he could attack him from behind. It was the coward's way of doing it, and he had no doubt that Dutch was a coward.

He heard the scream upstairs and it being cut off. Wesley was looking at a shelf when he saw it, or he might have missed the small movement. Going to the shelf, he bit down hard on the tarp that was there and knew he had Dutch as soon as the man screamed.

Pulling him out, Wesley felt something hit him twice before he was able to get the hand that held the gun. The snap of bone and the spray of blood startled him, but Wesley didn't let go as the hand with the gun left Dutch's arm. Slamming his large paw into the middle of Dutch's chest, Wesley held him down while the man screamed out in pain.

Penny, can you hear me? She moaned, and he'd never heard a better sound. *Honey, I need you to sit up if you can. Please? I'm right here, and I've got Dutch.*

She sat up, and he could see the large cut on the side of her head. Again, he had to remind himself not to go to her. If he let Dutch go now, he might get away. Watching her as he held down Dutch, she stared at him for a full minute before saying his name.

It's me, love. I've come to get you. She cried then, telling him that she loved him so much. *I love you. So much. Come here and touch my cat for me, so he can know you're all right.*

Penny stood up, but she wasn't steady on her feet. She held tightly onto the bench beside him and kicked Dutch three times in the head, yelling at him for hurting her and Emmie.

"Where is she? Did someone get her to the hospital?" Wesley didn't know for sure, but he didn't want to tell her that she was much more important than Emmie was. He told her she was on the way there now. "Good. This piece of shit shot her twice. I thought for sure she was— Oh Wesley, I'm so glad to see you here. I'm going to fucking kill this bastard."

He nearly laughed. She'd been so sad one second, then she was hot mad the next. He supposed it had to do with stress, but he loved her all the more for it. Telling her she needed to get the gun, he laughed when she reacted.

"This isn't funny. You should have told me there was a hand still on it." She laughed, and he knew it was stress then. "I just thought of something. Will it be considered suicide if I use his finger to shoot the fucking bastard?"

Sawyer came down just as she was kicking Dutch again. Wesley rubbed his head over Penny when she was told to sit down; the medics were there for her. Sawyer kicked Dutch too when he moved past him to give the medics more room.

"She's fine. I didn't kill her. Someone has to come here and help me. I'm bleeding really bad. I'm gonna die here. That cat there, it took my hand off. Can someone put some ice on it? They'll have to attach it when I get to the hospital." Dutch seemed to be unaware that he was being arrested. It was then that Wesley smelled the coke on him. "I'm bleeding here. Doesn't anyone care?"

Everyone in the basement told him *no* at the same time. Sawyer didn't cuff him. Penny made a comment about cuffing him up with one leg and one arm. Wesley went to sit next to her while the team saw to her head.

"Now is the time to change her, Wesley, if you want. She's going to be a great deal better at healing if you do." He asked Penny what she wanted. Her sing-song "Yes yes yes" had them all laughing again. "This is the strangest call I've been on in a while. I'm thinking that if you give her a couple of smaller bites when I get her on the gurney, she'll be all right once we get to the hospital. However, she'll have to hang out there for a few days."

"Do it, Wesley. Make me your cat bitch." He didn't have to be asked twice. With everyone watching them, Wesley bit Penny once in the belly, and that seemed to be all it took. He'd been giving her his blood since they'd been sleeping together, and that had more than likely saved her from being out right now. "I love you, Wesley Beasley. You are my wittle baby kitty."

"Either she's drunk, or she hit her head harder than we thought." He had to agree with his brothers. "I've never seen her so loopy. Have you, Wesley Beasley?" Another thing he'd never live down, he thought. Yet he didn't care.

It turned out she had hit her head hard. Just to make it look good, they put in staples to her head until they could stop the bleeding and get her X-rayed at the hospital. They also refrained from giving her any medication just in case someone had slipped her something while at the house.

They wrapped up Dutch's hand and put it in a plastic sheath. No one wanted to get the blood on them, so they were being extra careful with it. Penny had been taken up the stairs just then, and he was nearly ready to follow her when Dutch pulled out a knife from his boot.

For as long as he lived, Wesley would never remember moving. One second he was on the second step up, being careful of the slickness on them, and the next, he was at Dutch's body, tossing him back against the floor and tearing into his chest. The knife Dutch had thrown had stuck in the wood, not an inch from Sawyer's head. If it had hit him, it would have taken out his eye. As it was, his brother fell backward and hit his head on the concrete floor.

No one moved for what seemed like an eternity, but as soon as he snarled at the medic that had told him to change Penny, they began checking out his brother. He was glad that Sawyer was out of it when he got out of the house.

Wesley made his way to the tree line and tossed up everything he had on his belly. The taste of blood was still in his mouth.

Wesley was still a cat when his dad found him. Dad asked him three times if he was all right before he was able to answer him. Then he had to hit him to get him to change. Dad turned his back to him as he shifted and changed. He wondered if him being covered in blood had made his dad as ill as it had made him.

"Your mom is fit to be tied. She didn't want anyone to be hurt, but she's mad that she didn't get to hurt one of them men." Wesley said he'd killed Dutch. "You feel bad about that?"

"No, sir. He hurt Penny." Dad turned and glanced at

him. "He hurt Sawyer too. He's going to have to go to the hospital."

"You're all alive, and that's all a man can hope for at the end of the day, I think. Gunner, he's gone home. He told your mom if anyone wanted him, they'd have to come to him. He's tuckered out." Wesley was pulling on a pair of shoes when he asked his dad if he'd said it like that. "You know durn good and well he didn't. I tell you, I don't know where my children got their potty mouths from. But today, I'm not going to fuss too much. You changed her, didn't you?"

"Yes, sir. She was close, anyway." He told his dad he was dressed. Instead of telling him they were headed someplace, his dad turned and hugged him tighter than he ever had before. "I love you too, Dad. With all my heart and soul, I love you so very much."

"I love you too, son—all of you. I'm gonna make sure I tell you that more often now. I had three of my boys out there in dangerous situations, and I decided I don't care for that very much. I know it was necessary, but I don't like it." Wesley told his dad he didn't much care for it either. "You remember that too. I love you, Wesley. I'm here for you too. We'll get you to the hospital now. That Penny, she's going to be upset if you're not there when she wakes up. You tell her I love her too. All my girls."

Once he was at the hospital, he was taken directly to the room Emmie was in. She had wanted to see him. After hugging him three times, she told him to tell Penny she loved her and would see her soon. He didn't tell her Penny had been hurt as well.

The wait to see Penny seemed to take forever. They had to make sure she was all right. They were, as he'd been, concerned she seemed to be drugged up. Once they came out to tell him she was all right, that as the medics had said, it was stress, he could go and see her. It took him five minutes to get her to stop crying before he was able to hold her.

"You saved me." He said that was his job. "Yes, it was, and you did a wonderful job of it. However, I don't want you to do it again. Unless I'm being kidnapped by a deranged idiot."

"They're all dead, but Tony." She said he'd been by to see her when she got to the ER. "Good. Do you remember anything after James took you from the house?"

"Not too much. Dutch hit me then, James did." He nodded and told her he loved her again. "I don't want to talk about it either. I do want to talk to you about having a baby. Soon. I don't want to wait another minute."

"All right, love. As soon as we can arrange it." Penny laid her head on his hand as he held hers. "You'll have to stay here for a couple of days. After that, we'll practice at making a baby. All right?"

"I love you. I love you so very much." She closed her eyes then. "I'm exhausted. They said since you changed me, I can rest, but boy, I'm tired."

He watched her all night, terrified that if he turned

away for even a second, someone would take her again. Wesley spoke to his family, telling them she was all right and resting. They promised they'd come to see her tomorrow. He was glad for that. Wesley wanted to spend time with her alone until she was better. Christ, it had been a nightmarish last few days.

Chapter 9

Penny was trying her best to be brave, but this was the most difficult thing she'd ever done. Going with her father to the place he was going to be living for the rest of his days was tearing her apart inside.

"This is the best place for me." She told him she knew that. "I'll get help in controlling my urges to kill myself, and I'll have doctors here all the time that will make sure I'm in control of the people here with me."

"I feel as if I'm only just getting to know you, and now I have to send you away." He hugged her again. It wasn't helping her to stop crying, but she'd not give up on this time with him for anything. "They said you have a phone in your room that you can call out whenever you want. You'll call, won't you?"

"Every day, if I can." She knew there were going to be times when it would be difficult for him. This place was going to do him so much good that she wanted him there as much as she wanted him home with her. "You can call me too, honey. I'm going to look forward to that."

Tony had slipped away sometime after James was killed. He didn't want to be the host any longer. So while he sat in his room, just staring at the wall, the others had taken a vote and elected someone to be the one in charge of decisions. It was Presley that had been voted in by the others.

They hadn't been close, Tony and James. However, Tony had been unable to deal with life after feeling responsible for the death of so many. He'd not been, of course. James had caused his own death by taking her. That was another reason he'd been willing to come here. The rest of them—seven total personalities, including Tony—needed to deal with the deaths as well.

"Your father-in-law is going to come and visit me and bring along Joe. I think this will be more fun than I've had in a while. Us old people need to have friends around, so when we don't answer our door, they know to come look for us."

The funny thing was that Presley claimed he was in his late eighties. But in reality, the man was only forty-six, the same age Tony was. It was one of the reasons he'd been voted as host. He had "lived" a lot longer than any of the others.

While she didn't have any idea how that worked, she was happy for them all. Sometimes it got confusing as to who she was talking to at any given time. For the most part, they would tell her who she was with when she asked. Penny had fallen in love with all of the others with her brother. The one that she had the most fun with was Joey.

Joey was the youngest of the seven and a jokester. She loved the fact that he could make her laugh about anything. Joey was also the one that dealt with stress by making the others laugh at whatever the stressor was. It would get them evened out again. Joey was only fifteen.

"They told us you'd be able to leave to come and visit us too. I do hope you'll be able to come to the house for Christmas and the other holidays." Presley told her he was looking forward to that more than anything. "I was worried you'd tell me you'd be safer here. I hope you know you'll be welcome anytime you want to visit."

"I know that. Even Wesley told me I could come around at planting time, and he'd show me how to drive the tractor. I think we'd enjoy that. He surely is a farmer, isn't he?" She laughed with Presley. "I've never seen a man so excited when a seed catalog comes in. He must have looked that thing over fifty times before the end of the day it arrived." She told him that he'd made a list. "Yes, I saw that. He said he has a system. That when the catalog comes in, he marks everything he wants. Then over the next few months, he pares it down. However, he did say that with his new tractor, he might well not have to pare it down that much. I guess it's much quicker than his old tractor. He called it Old Man. Appropriate, I guess. He said it was older than his father."

"They'd been nursing it along for years. Getting the new tractor has saved them so much time. I'm so proud of him for going around helping other families out. Did he tell you he's going to help with the upgrade to the football field this spring? He's going to use some of the equipment that came with the tractor that he's not been able to use yet." Presley said she looked to be excited about it as well. "I am. It makes me happy when he gets like that. He loves me."

"Of course he does. You're a wonderful wife for him. The two of you, you're perfect for each other." She told him she thought so as well. "Good. You have so much more than any other family just starting out. I don't mean the tangible things, but love — laughter too. It does this old man a great deal of good to hear you two putting your heads together in fun."

There was that old man again. When Presley was speaking to one of the doctors who was going to be doing his care, she watched him. He did look like an older man, from the sandals that he wore with white knee socks to the big sloppy sweater he was forever in. To her, that was a hint that it was Presley. He slipped the sweater on as he did his personality.

"They want me to check out a couple of rooms they have open. The doctor said I could take you with me." She stood up when he did, even going as far as to helping him move. "I know this body is young and fit, but I'm not sure what to do with all that energy it has. It's hard for others to believe I don't get around better."

"I don't care what they think so long as you're comfortable." He said he was, but he did feel old. "Then I'd say that to hell with what the others around you think. You are perfect the way you are."

The first room he was shown was very girly. Not just feminine, but like a child had lived there and had loved pink. The furniture wasn't yet taken out, but she could see that someone had even painted the wooden frame pink as well. He turned it down right away.

"There are no female personalities, Mr. Presley?" Presley told him not that he'd seen. "That's good to know. You'll let us know if that changes, won't you? We're here to treat all of you, not just the one we will see most."

She liked that about this place. It was a safe haven for men and women like Presley. Penny wasn't sure they believed him, but they were kind enough not to treat him like a freak when all he wanted to do was help himself.

The second room looked like it had been designed just for him. While the furniture was taken out of this suite of rooms, the wallpaper, as well as the carpet, was a nice shade of blue. Even the windows in the living part of it looked out over the back of the place. While they were looking around, a few deer made their way out into the little area. She was checking out the bathroom when she heard from Raven.

Did you know the place he's staying at is one of the places I own? She asked her if that was all right. *Yes. I didn't know it was part of a land deal I made some years ago. Had I known, I would have been taking care that it was updated better than it was. There are a couple of work orders here that have been in a file for about four years. Can you do me a favor and have a look at the kitchen area? It says here that there is a common kitchen for them to use when they wish to cook for themselves.*

Sure. Presley has a microwave as well as a small refrigerator in the room he's going to be taking. We've been told he could swap those out, at his own expense, for larger models. I think I'd like to make that happen for him. Raven asked her to check on that as well. *I will. Something I did notice, and it might not be a big deal, there aren't enough wheelchairs to go around. Not that many need them here, but there is only one chair for the two that do. They have to be taken around, then the staff goes back for the other person.*

I'll look into that as well. Also, there is supposed to be a doctor on staff all the time. I'm looking to make sure that is happening. Penny asked if she wanted her to tell her anything else that she might notice. *I would love for you to do that. As I said, I'm just being made aware that I own the facility. I honestly thought it was just the land, but apparently, the building and the things that go on there are my responsibility as well.*

Presley decided he would take this room. The only thing now was getting him furniture that he'd like to bring in. They had already talked about things such as dressers and the like. Presley wanted new. He didn't want anything to associate himself with the others. Penny didn't blame him at all for that. She was going to make arrangements for the things he'd picked out yesterday to be brought in and set up.

The common area wasn't much more than a single microwave, as well as another small dorm-sized fridge. The tables around the room needed to be replaced. Very few of them were without a small piece of paper under the legs to keep them steady. Penny told Raven about that as well as the kitchen.

I'd say this kitchen hasn't seen a good cleaning for a long time. Raven asked her what she thought the issue was. *I would say it's the staff rather than anything else. There are four women and one man in the room, and they're smoking around a table, not a foot from food that is lying out on the counter yet to be put away. It looks like breakfast stuff.*

It's going on two o'clock. Don't they cook lunch? She said she didn't know, but it didn't look like it. *I wonder what the deal with that is. All right. I'm adding it to my list. Christ, this couldn't have been timed better. Thank you so much for helping me out with this.*

Penny did her own kind of snooping and question asking while there. Presley seemed to be enjoying their sleuthing too. He would ask a question of one of the people staying there, and she would keep a running monologue with Raven. They were having more luck with the clients there than they were the doctor. Plus, they were having a good time.

Well, I thought you'd like to know what Presley has

uncovered. *The doctor showing the two of us around is the only doctor on staff. He is called in when they need him, even in the middle of the night. On occasion, he spends the night here, as he's here mostly during the day. Doctor Bench — Jerry is his first name — has been trying to keep up with everything going on around here. I have to tell you, you'd never know he's being overworked by talking to him. He's as upbeat as Joey can be.* Raven wrote down his name and said she'd look into that as well. *There are a couple of things that you might put at the top of your list. There are no activities here. The few board games are things that children would play — no decks of cards. We've been told that twice now. No trips to the store for them either. The one bus they have that would take them places is working, but no one here will drive it.*

That's strange. According to the website that was recently updated, there are day trips once a month as well as trips to the town for groceries and lunch out if they want. Raven laughed. *I have a warehouse full of games they can have — decks of cards, as well as poker chips. I bought a hotel once, and they had this entire floor of rooms filled with things like that. I'll have someone look into bringing them over.*

By the time she was ready to leave, she was sure that Raven had too much on her plate. Penny should have known better. As they were getting into their car, Jerry, the doctor, came out to get them. Raven apparently had given him a call.

"The new owner called. She told me that the two of you are sisters. I'm sorry if I might have sounded too bitchy earlier." Penny told him he hadn't, but without Raven knowing, there couldn't be any changes to the place. "You have no idea how embarrassed I am, but also glad. You and your brother, you've really come through for the people here. Thank you."

"You're so very welcome." She started to leave, but he stopped her once more. "Is there something I can help you with?"

"Yes. Raven said she was coming up here in the morning to have a look around. She made me promise I wouldn't try and hold back on showing her things. I know you were only trying to help us here, but—and this is no come on, I promise you—but would you mind accompanying her tomorrow? You have told her things I didn't notice about this place. She also is bringing a crew with her, she told me, to start fixing some of the things that have been neglected."

"She's a wonderful person and likes for people to tell her straight up what they need. Don't be surprised if she's a little pushy." Presley told him not to be afraid of her. "Yes, good point. Raven is very forward thinking, and can peel the paint off a barn when she's pissed off."

Jerry was laughing when they left the second time. She would come up with Raven tomorrow if only to see that Presley was set up. But she would enjoy, she thought, seeing Raven working. She had a feeling everyone in the place was going to be running for cover before she was finished with the place.

~*~

Gunner was sitting on his deck when his dad showed up. Dad told him that he'd been at the front door for a while and decided to see if he was back here. Being offered and turning down a beer, Dad sat down in the chair next to him. Neither of them spoke for a while before he finally asked his dad why he was there.

"I've been thinking about something. Nothing bad, but it's been preying on my mind for a couple of days. What did you do in the service?" Gunner took a drink of his beer and thought about the answer. "While you're thinking on that, I want to know if I have to keep reading the paper to figure out where you might be going next."

"I can answer one of those questions. The other you're not going to like the answer to." Dad nodded. "You shouldn't read the paper, Dad. There are all kinds of falsehoods there that will upset you. Most of it is true, but a lot of it isn't. If you want to know if I'm in danger, then the answer would be yes. Every time I leave here and before."

"I see. You know, when you told us you were home for good, I knew there was more to that than just you being out of the service. You're still a serviceman, aren't you, son?" He said he was. "Do you...are you still doing the same job you were doing before you came home? I'm thinking I don't want to know what you were doing for the country."

"You don't. And yes, I'm still helping out with jobs for the country. I'm not careful either if that was going to be your next question." Dad just looked at him, then looked out over the woods behind his house. "Dad, I'm not a good person. I've been doing things I'm not proud of for a very — "

"Don't you dare say that. Don't you dare tell me you're not a good person. You are doing a job no one else wants, and that is keeping us safe. I'm sure there is a lot of blood on your hands. I would say there is a great deal of it, but that doesn't make you a bad person, Gunner. That makes you a good soldier." Gunner felt his eyes fill with tears, something that hadn't happened to him in a good long time. "You hurt, I'm sure of that. Hurt for the things you've had to do. That's what makes you think you're not a good person. But you are. I raised you, and I know you're the best of your mother and me. All of you are. Don't even think that again, Gunner. Please."

"I love you, Dad."

He said that he loved him as well and patted him on the hand.

Gunner had to breathe in and out several times before he could speak again. It wasn't hurt that he was feeling, but love. It filled his heart up so much it was overflowing into parts of his body that had been darkened for a long time. "Since Sasha made me an immortal like she did the rest of you, it's kept me safer."

"Have I almost lost you a few times, Gunner?" He didn't answer him, but he supposed that was answer enough for his dad. "When I was a younger man, I wanted to join the army. It was something all young men did then, and I was ready to sign up and be one of the ones that kept this nation safe. But back then, they didn't allow shifters in the service. I suppose a few of them lied about it and were able to get by. I couldn't lie about it to them. They knew who I was and what I was before I'd signed up. You see, my mother did that. She was dead set against me going overseas to fight, and let it *slip*, she told me, that I wasn't human. I don't know to this day if I'm happy she did that or upset with her. I'd have not had you boys had I gone, and that right there is enough of a reason for me."

"Then, I will be thankful for her doing it every day for the rest of my life." Dad nodded and finally leaned back in his chair. "I hope you and Mom don't expect me to have a mate. I mean, she might well be out there, but I'm not a person that would be easy on a person. Especially a woman. I just don't want you to get your hopes up too much."

"I think whoever is out there for you, Gunner—and she is out there—she'll be able to put up with anything you can dish out to her." Dad laughed. "I mean, look at your brother Sawyer. He sure did hit the jackpot on finding someone to put up with him, didn't he?"

They both laughed and seemed to settle down for a little while. When the deer started to come out to enjoy the salt licks he'd put out for them, they sat there in companionable silence for a long time. As it started to get darker and cooler out, the two of them swapped stories about the others, telling tales that were as funny and sad as they were at the time they happened.

"How will I know when you're out again?" Gunner asked his dad if he wanted him to tell him. "I'm not sure, now that I think about it. I'll just worry until you return. No. I don't want to know. I just decided that. But if you need us, you know you only have to reach out, and we'll be there for you."

"I know that, Dad. I've always known that." Dad asked him if he came to see his brothers often when he was away. "I do. Mostly Sawyer. I don't know why, but he patches me up if I need it and doesn't ask that many questions. Before you get upset about that, no, I don't usually need patching up. But on occasion, I need just a cut or something cleaned out."

He could tell his dad didn't believe him. Not the part about him being hurt, but the part where he only needed a small amount of work done on him. The times he'd been hurt and had to suffer through it before he could find a place to shift were many. Gunner had scars from the few times he'd been injured without being able to shift. Dad changed the subject then, for which Gunner was grateful.

"I'm thinking of Christmas a lot here lately. It's going to be a good one. Lots of kids around to play with and spoil. More women around to keep your mom happy. She sure does like having the others around to talk to." Gunner let him talk—there wasn't anything he could add to the conversation anyway. "I want to make this one a new start to our lives. Go big, I'm thinking. A big tree with ornaments on every branch. So many gifts under the tree that there isn't much room for us to walk around the room. And the kids. I want them there the entire time. You know, some families let the kids open gifts first then send them off to play? That's not right. I want them there forever. And I will make it happen too."

"If the wives keep coming and children with them, it's going to be a huge mess once we start on the gifts, Dad. Do you think that'll be all right with Mom?" Dad laughed and said it was her idea. "Figures. Mom is in seventh heaven with all these children around. The other day I saw her with Pip. That kid has her wrapped around her little finger tighter than any of us ever did, I think."

"I think you might be right about that. The other day I saw Sawyer with Raven. She's getting around well for being that far along. But your brother is a mess. He worries about every little thing she does." They both enjoyed a good laugh at his brother's expense. "I tell you, Gunner, that man is going to have a complete breakdown when that child is born. I cannot wait to see it."

At a little before nine, Dad said he'd better go home. They'd spent a good four hours talking, and Gunner felt better than he had in the last few days. He wondered if he could have Dad or one of the others come over often to push away the depression.

Getting up, he picked up the two beer bottles he'd emptied and took them into the house. Beer didn't do much for him. It didn't give him any kind of high like it did some. He just got used to drinking it over water when he'd been out of the country. To him, it was safer and cleaner than water. He didn't think he'd get anything from drinking water someplace else, but why take the chance, he told himself.

There still wasn't much in the way of furniture in his home. Holly had given him a lot of pieces, but so far, all he'd done with them was put them in the rooms he'd thought they'd go in and not bothered with setting anything up. He'd get around to it, he told himself.

Going to the bedroom he'd claimed as his own, he grinned when he realized he'd forgotten his mattress had arrived. Not that he'd put the bed together yet, but the mattress and the box springs were leaning against the wall for him to use. Gunner decided he'd have to get sheets before he used the bed.

Gunner was nearly asleep when he realized what the day after tomorrow was. Thanksgiving. He had plans that he couldn't break. His mother had badgered him into telling her what they were. Going to the veteran's shelter was something he'd not ever been able to do before, and he was excited to do it. She told him he was a good boy.

"You do know I'm not a boy anymore, don't you, Mom? I mean, I've been voting and everything for over ten years now." She said he'd always be a boy to her. "All right. If that's the way you want to think about it. But I won't be there for lunch. I really want to do this. There are a lot of vets there, and I feel I owe them to help out."

"Well, of course, you do." She asked him who she contacted to help. "I'll mention it to the rest of the family, and perhaps they'll want to help too."

He didn't tell her she didn't have to do that. Gunner thought it might upset her. Besides, there was never enough help at these things. They nearly cried when he asked if he could come and help. Giving her the phone number of the person to contact, he was sure that every one of his family would be there, dishing out food for a wonderful cause.

Closing his eyes again, he thought about having a mate. It scared him to think someone would love him. Not that Gunner thought no one loved him, but this would be someone he would sleep with. The nightmares were too much for him at times. He couldn't imagine what it would do for someone sleeping beside him.

Only time would tell, he supposed. For all he knew, she could be more badass than he was. Laughing a little, he rolled to his back and let sleep take him under. Tomorrow was going to be a big day, and he wanted to be able to not fall asleep while handing out scoops of mashed potatoes.

Chapter 10

"If you say that to me one more time, I'm going to have someone bury you in an anthill and leave you there to be eaten alive. I told you, several times, I do not want anything to eat. I'm fine right here where I am." The doctor just stared at her. "Go away. I have better things to do than to have you huffing at me this early in the morning."

"I think I might have mentioned to you several times, Captain, that this will be the only meal served today. No one has time to cater to your needs when there are so many that actually need help." Hodge glared at him, telling him again that she'd not asked anyone for special treatment. "That's right. You want to just lie in your bed or in that contraption you're in and wallow in your self-pity. Well fine. You can die here for all I care."

"Nice bedside manner, dick head." He left her there, slamming the door like a child would do when they didn't get their way. Hodge rolled her wheelchair to the window and looked out over the water that was as stagnant as her mind was.

Hodge had been here for almost six weeks now. After she left here, she would go to a rehabilitation center, where they'd work on getting her muscles strengthened again. Then after that, who knew. They'd told her as they were transferring her from the ship she'd been on to get put back together that her career as a grunt was finished. She was as washed up at this job as she was at anything she'd set her heart on.

Smiling to herself, she realized she was wallowing in her own self-pity. Not liking that any more than she did Doctor Fucktard, she leaned her head on the back of her chair and closed her eyes. Reliving her last day on the ground haunted her even in her waking hours.

It had taken them three days of grueling weather to make it across the dark desert. Traveling at night and burying down during the day was hot work, but it was safer for her and her five men. The six of them had been working together for the last sixteen months. Two of them were going home in less than a month. It hurt her that none of them were going home in the style they had counted on after that third morning. At night, they would talk about what they were going to do when they got home.

"I'm going to find me a woman and fuck her until neither of us can move." They laughed, never thinking of her as anything but one of the men. "Then I'm going to take a shower for two whole days, just to make sure I have all my nooks and crannies cleaned up. Isn't that what you call them, Captain? Nooks and crannies?"

"Bits and pieces. I suppose you could use that term too, Markley—we've seen what you have to offer a woman." That, of course, was the comment they were waiting on—her to put one or all of them down with a slick insult. "Get to sleep, dumbasses. We have a long night in front of us, and I don't want any of you saying you didn't get enough beauty sleep. Becks, you take the first watch."

The empty building they'd been in since arriving at the little town had running water as well as some dark corners during the day. None of them would use the water to even clean up their hands. They'd been around the block enough to know that things could be put in anything and cause death to the soldier.

She was making sure they were all out of sight and that Becks was out where he could keep an eye on them when they rested. Night work was what they were here for. The sooner they were able to get it done, the quicker she could get back to her base.

The touch to her shoulder was all that was needed to pull her from the nightmarish dream she was having and to bring down the person who had awakened her. Hodge was hurting, her back especially. Hodge didn't know where the broken cup came from, nor the woman beneath her, but she didn't move when she started speaking to her.

"I'm sorry." Hodge wanted to move, to tell the person

she'd hurt that she was sorry, but she couldn't. Moving now would not only make her pass out, but Doc Fucktard would come back in and shoot her up with meds. "I'm so sorry. I should have known better. I'm going to move."

"Don't." The woman nodded. "I cannot move yet. Don't let the doctor touch me. He's an idiot."

"My name is Sippy. Sippy Bishop. I'm here with my family, and one of the others here said you didn't come out of your room much. I was bringing you something to eat." She was babbling, Hodge knew that. But moving now would make them both hurt. "I'm a tiger, honey. Anything that happened here, it's not going to be—"

"Soldier, what the fuck are you doing to my mother? I'm Major Bishop, and you'd better be heeding my warning." The voice was full of authority. The woman told the person behind her to hush up. "Get up off my mother before I pick you up by your ass and toss you across the room. Did you hear me? What is your name?"

"Captain Andrew Hodge, sir. I can't move. I can't move until the pain kills me. Hopefully, that'll be soon." She heard the change in his voice as soon as he bent at her level. He asked her where she hurt. "I'm injured everywhere. If I move, you might as well kill me here. If you don't, that fucking doctor is going to. He thinks that whatever happened over there is all in my mind. That I fed my men to the wolves, so to speak."

"Mom, I'm going to go and get someone to help out." The woman beneath her, Sippy, told him not to get the doctor. "I won't. But Quincy is here, and he might be able to help her out."

When the shadow that had fallen over her left, she closed her eyes and tried to breathe her way through the pain. Looking at Sippy, she told her again how sorry she was. When she smiled at her, Sippy asked her if her name was really Andrew.

"My mother. She was fifteen when she had me and didn't know how to spell Andrew in a girly way. I don't know if there is any way, but that's what ended up on my birth certificate." Hodge wasn't sure that was important at the moment. "The man here, Major Bishop, he's pissed at me, and I might be able to have him knock me out with his fists. You think?"

"He'd better not if he knows what's good for him. There they are now. Quincy, could you please help this young lady out? She's in a great deal of pain." He said he was going to have to wait on his bag. "Oh, good. I'm glad you're prepared. Gunner, dear, could you please go and tell Raven that the doctor here needs his butt handed to him? Anyone can see that this happened and isn't in her mind."

Hodge didn't know if Gunner had left or which of the men she'd been referring to. The doctor asked her if she had any allergies. When she told him only to pain, she felt the coolness of a wipe on her arm, then the pinch of the needle. The meds circled around her head quickly, making her slightly dizzy, then she was out.

The pain brought her awake enough to know she was being moved. It didn't matter that she begged them to leave her alone, she found herself in the bed once again. Waking up a second time, she heard the angry voice of Doc Fucktard and a woman. Whoever she was, Hodge thought for sure she could teach her a few curse words.

The room was bright with light when she woke up again. Her body ached just a little, so she didn't try moving it. Hodge thought that if the pain was still sleeping, she'd not wake it up just yet.

There was an IV in her arm. Two bags were hanging from the pole was attached to the bed. One of them was clear, the other a piss yellow. Still careful not to move too much, she looked around the room with her eyes. That was when she realized she was in an actual hospital and not the vet center where she'd been before.

It took Hodge three tries before she was able to get enough spit in her mouth to form a word. Longer still to get the words she wanted to say out of her mouth. The room seemed to move a bit too much for her, so she closed her eyes. When she opened them, being ordered to no less, she looked at the face of the man standing over her.

"Gunner." She nodded, still unsure who he was. "Major Bishop. We spoke four days ago when you were hurting."

"On your mom." He nodded and grinned at her. "You're not charming, so go away. I'd like to die in peace if you'd not mind."

"I do mind, actually. And you're not going to die. Not anymore." Closing her eyes when he moved, she asked him what he was talking about. "How are you feeling? My brother, Quincy, had you brought to a larger hospital after he read over your chart. Raven, my sister-in-law, a ball-buster too, had Doctor Fletcher fired." She asked him who that was. "Doc Fucktard."

"He's an idiot." Gunner laughed again. "Why am in not at the vet's center? I was supposed to be learning some skills there that I could use when they put me out to pasture. For that matter, why the hell are you here? Don't you have some Rambo shit you have to work on or something?"

"Not today. I was able to pull your work record and what happened that brought you here. I assume Fucktard never read it. Or if he did, he just wrote it off as a lie. Whatever his excuses were, he's out of a job, and the veteran's association is looking into other accusations against him." Hodge wondered why he'd care, but didn't ask him. He was looking over a menu from a restaurant she'd never heard of. "I'm hungry. How about you?"

"I know you outrank me. How that works, I'm not really sure, but what the fuck are you doing here? Seriously? No, I'm not hungry. I'm hurting." She moved but didn't feel the pain she normally did. "Well, I usually hurt like a fucking train ran over me. But that doesn't mean I'm any less curious as to why— Something isn't right. You did something, or your brother did. Your mother, Sippy. She said something while I was hurting her. She— You're a cat."

"Yes." She could have gotten up and socked him in the face. But she thought he'd only laugh at her. "How are you feeling? Better, I'm assuming."

"You fucking bastard. You gave me your blood, didn't you? And for you to be able to do that, you'd have to— Mother fuck. You think I'm your mate. No fucking way. There is no fucking way that I'm going to be a— Mother fuck, I hate you right now."

The door opened, and there stood a woman and two men. The men she knew, the woman she didn't.

"I guess you told her." The woman introduced herself as Raven Bishop. "These men are people you know, I guess. Major Wilkerson and Major Partisan are here to speak to you about your stay at the veteran's center and the doctor that was treating you." Hodge told them to get out. "They need to know what sort of charges you're going to press against the—"

"Get the fuck out of this room. Right now." No one moved until Gunner stood up. "You, sit. You're going to tell me what the hell you did."

"You're a cat too. It was that or let you die. And since you *are* my mate, I didn't think that was going to work for me." She asked why he'd do such a thing without her permission. "I told you. It was that, or you were going to die from the infection that was racing over your body when the doctor at the center decided you weren't worth his time."

"What sort of someone is he that decided I should die?" He moved toward the door and turned to look at her. "This isn't finished. I'm not going to be your slave, Major Bishop. You might well have found a Deb to mate with rather than me. I got nothing. I have no career, no money, and I certainly don't have time to try and figure out something so fucking lame as being a cat. What sort of cat am I, anyway?"

"White Bengal tiger." He moved. It was so quick she didn't see him do it, even though she was looking right at him. Gunner was so close to her that she could almost taste his mouth. "I don't want a slave as a mate. I don't care what you have or don't have either. But as of the moment you took your last breath as a human, you became the one person in this world that I would gladly die for."

"I'm not worthy of you, Gunner." He looked at her, deep into her eyes, and she felt so exposed she wanted to cover up. There wasn't any way for her to cover herself deep into her soul. "I don't know why I'm still alive."

"Because you were meant to be mine." He stood up then, and the two men were gone. The only people left were Raven and Gunner. "This is Raven, my sister-in-law. She's going to make sure you're taken care of while you're here. Which won't be all that much longer."

"I don't need you to go around making things better for me. I'm fine to do that all by myself." Gunner just grunted, and Raven reminded her that she'd been near death when they had arrived. "Perhaps that is precisely what I wanted to happen."

Gunner threw back his head and laughed. Glancing at Raven, she looked as shocked with his reaction as Hodge was. For some reason, she had a feeling he didn't laugh all that much. Or at least this hard. When he was finished with his mirth, he leaned down and kissed her on the mouth. After that, he walked out the door, leaving the two of them alone. She looked at Raven.

"You've made him happy." Hodge told her she didn't know what she was talking about. "Perhaps you don't. But you have. I've never seen him laugh like that, much less kiss someone. Well, that's probably a good thing. But you've made him happy, and as far as I'm concerned, you can have anything you want from now on."

"If I were to tell you I don't want to be here, to be his mate, could you fix that?" Raven just laughed and went to the door. The two men out there, dressed in their blues, came in and told her they were going to ask her a few questions. She looked at Raven again. "Why are you doing this?"

"I'm not. Gunner did. He did it mostly for you, but there were four other soldiers there at the center that were not being treated either. You were one of the lucky ones. One of the other men died, and the other two might not make it. Doc Fletcher is in prison for crimes against the government. You, I hope, are going to be able to make it so he stays there."

Hodge answered the questions put to her. Raven never left her. It took her a few minutes to understand why. Two men in the room with a mated cat would spell their deaths. So, she put up with the questions and the men in order to have some quiet time. She needed to think about what the hell was going on.

~*~

Gunner found his dad just where he thought he would, down in the cafeteria talking. It didn't matter that the people he was talking to had jobs. Dad would talk to anyone if he was given half a chance. Gunner sat down at one of the tables and waited for him to get whatever he'd gotten paid for.

"They sure do have some good food here, don't they? I've never had such an array of things to eat before. How's that pretty mate of yours?" He told him she was pissed. "I don't usually care for that sort of description, but I'm thinking it's about perfect for her. What she the most upset about? The changing, or that you and she are mates?"

"I'd say it's about even across the board." Dad laughed, and Gunner smiled. "They're talking to her about the center and the doctor there. Also, they're going to see if they can work in a couple of questions about what happened over there that got her so shot up."

"You do know that isn't going to make her any happier with you than she is now, don't you, son?" He nodded and took the bowl of grapes from his dad's tray when they were offered to him. "You told me yesterday that you read over her file. I'm assuming you aren't supposed to be able to do that. Not the way you did it."

"Not really. I could request it, but that would take too long. I knew the doctor would have a copy of it in his office, so I made a copy of it and left it there. His was redacted, but I got what I needed out of it." Dad asked him what that meant. "Someone blacked out what they didn't want him to know, which was quite a lot of information. But I've read these kinds of reports before and know how to get what I want out of them. She was one of six people that were attacked that night. The other five men in her team were murdered, their throats slit. She was lucky enough to have been able to wake up and fight her attacker off before she killed him."

"You said she was a good leader. Can you tell me what she might have been doing over there that would have had her with a team?" Gunner didn't answer his dad. "I thought that is what you'd tell me. From all accounts at that center, that doctor had her targeted for some reason. Do you know the answer to why he'd do that?"

"I don't know. But I'm going to find out. Hodge has no family left. She was in an orphanage since she was about a year old. I have a couple of men looking into what happened to have her end up there." Dad asked him if he wanted to wait on her to tell him. "She might not know either. According to her enlistment paperwork, she doesn't even know who her parents are, much less what happened to them."

"Well, that's sad." Gunner didn't know if it was sad or fortuitous for the woman. "We gonna have to call her Hodge? Your mom told me she said her first name is Andrew. With what you said about her family being dead, I have a feeling Hodge made that part up."

"I'm assuming so as well. But on her birth certificate she used to enlist, it does have her first name as Andrew. Her middle name is Graceland. Andrew Graceland Hodge. I'm sure Hodge came about when she became a soldier. It would have been something she adopted while coming up through the ranks." Dad said she didn't look like any of those names. "No. She doesn't look like an Andrew at all."

"You sweet on her?" Gunner looked at his dad and asked him what he meant. "I don't know, son. You like her? She seems a little rough around the edges. Nothing that you're not used to, I guess, but she sure has a way with words."

He laughed. Gunner had laughed more in the last few days than he had since forever, he thought. Just as he was going to tell his dad that, he felt a tentative touch to his mind.

I'm assuming since you changed me into a cat that I can contact you, correct? He said she could, then asked her what people called her when she wasn't in the service. *I have no idea since that's all I've been called since I can remember. One of the men here wants to know where I'm going after this. Since I don't have a pot to piss in, I'm assuming you might have someplace for me to stay until we get this settled between us.*

The only way I can think of to settle this between us is to have a night of passionate lovemaking. Or we could do something else if you're into that. She told him to fuck off, and he laughed again. *Yes, I have an address for you to use. Since Raven is there, tell her to give them mine. I don't own a cell phone; they'll get you into trouble when you're out —*

I heard one — that night. A cell phone went off while we were resting. He didn't interrupt her thoughts. *We had all just bedded down except for Becks. He had first watch. I heard a twittering sound, like a cellphone going off, and it woke me.*

It more than likely is what saved your life. I'm assuming you've not been questioned about that night overly much. She told him how she'd not been bothered that she knew of. *I found in your records that Doc Fucktard sent them away whenever the army came to question you. Perhaps that has a little to do with it.*

That sounds like something he'd do. He thought I was just making it up. The fact that five other men lost their lives wasn't figured into his picture, I guess. She didn't speak, and Gunner wondered if she was thinking about something else. *Raven said to tell you that you need to get some furniture in your house set up. While I don't have any idea why she would know about your living arrangements, perhaps she can fuck off too.*

Gunner told his dad what was going on. He told him he could contact the leap and see if they could help him out by getting things set up. Gunner told him he didn't even have any sheets or the knowledge of how to go about getting any.

"I guess you would sort of get into the habit of shopping for things like that. I'll tell you what. When your mom gets here, we'll take a little shopping trip to the stores here in town and get some. Somebody at the house can figure out what sizes we need."

They both looked up when they heard someone yelling for them.

Molly, Raven's daughter, hugged them both and sat next to him at the table. She was going on about how she'd yet to meet his mate, that the men in there were taking her time up. Dad went to get her a Danish when she said she was starving.

Molly looked at Gunner. "I have a question for you. You don't have to answer me, but you do know that not answering a question is really answering it." Gunner told her that answering questions could also give her nightmares. "I bet coming from you, they would. But it's nothing like that. I was wondering if you could help me with a school project. It's about veterans and how they're treated. It's for my social interaction class. Not social studies, but interaction."

"Perhaps you should talk to Hodge." She asked him if that was what he was going to call his mate. "That's all I know of that she goes by."

"I'm going to call her Aunt Andi. Whoever named her Andrew is a dummy head." Gunner laughed, and Molly looked up at him. She was the oldest nine-year-old he knew. "You need to laugh more often, Uncle Gunner. It makes you look so much younger."

"So, are you saying I look like an old man?" Molly touched her small hand to his cheek. She studied him intently until she turned away. "Do you see something you're afraid of, Molly?"

"No. I see something you're afraid of. You're afraid of Aunt Andi, and what her being your mate means, I think. You're also happy, but mostly afraid." Gunner didn't know what to say. She was right on both accounts. "See? I told you not answering was the same as answering. Can I tell you something? You should treat her the same way you might want someone to treat you. Don't treat her like a pretty thing. She doesn't need that. No flowers either. It will make her sad to know they'll eventually die."

"How do you know this? You've not even met her." Molly said she could figure things out on her own sometimes. "I think you might be right about her. She's had a very difficult life."

"That's what Grandma Sippy told me. She told me that Aunt Andi is hurting too, where no one can see it. I think you have that same kind of pain, don't you?" He nodded at her. "Yes. I thought so. Maybe the two of you can figure each other out and have a better life by it. I know I'd like to hear you laugh more than you do. I'm betting she doesn't laugh all that much either."

When Dad came back with a carton of white milk for him and the Danish for Molly, he told them about the lunch menu that was coming up in a couple of hours. As

Dad went on about having a meatball sub, Gunner touched Hodge's mind to see how she was doing. Her anger was like a blast of heat tossed at him. He carefully asked her what he could do for her.

These people need to get their heads out of their asses. Do you suppose either of these men here has ever stepped onto a battlefield? Have ever had anyone shoot at them? Fuckers are questioning my bunking down in an empty building. Where the hell else did they expect us to go? To a nice bed and breakfast that would have wake up call for us? Mother fuckers. She growled low. *I need a new word for idiots. Mother fucker is used to death. What do you use when you're pissed off at someone?*

Cock sucker. Douche canoe. It depends on the moment. Sometimes I can mix it up a little, and that usually helps. I'm here in the cafeteria with my dad. Can I bring you up anything – from the menu – that you'd like to eat? She asked if he was hinting she couldn't hit people with it. *That's exactly what I was saying. They have a nice Danish here if you want. My niece thinks it's good.*

I don't like sugary things. Donuts are the rave, but I can't stand them. Cake or pie either. I like fruit. He filed that information in his mind for later. *Can you see if they have a gallon of white milk for me? Not that much, but a nice carton or two would be fantastic.*

He told his dad what he was going to get for Hodge. When he stood up to go get them, he heard Molly telling his dad that she was going to call her Aunt Andi. They were agreeing it sounded better than Hodge.

Gunner snagged her a few bowls of fresh fruit that were laid out, as well as the milk. There was bottled water, what he preferred over most drinks, as well as some sandwiches. Getting three roast beef ones, he stacked them up on his tray to take to her room. Paying for what he had, he watched as Dad picked up two hot teas, as well as some slices of pizza. Dad could eat his weight in snack food every meal.

Taking the food up in the elevator, as soon as the doors opened to her floor, Gunner knew Hodge was pissed. He was reasonably sure everyone on the floor knew it too. Walking into the room without knocking, he saw her standing toe to toe with Raven, and neither of them noticed him coming in.

Sitting down, he arranged the food on her tray as he thought about what she was saying to Raven. Gunner wasn't going to get in the middle of it. He wasn't stupid. Women, he knew, could fight dirtier than men. They were also unforgiving of men who tried to break up their arguing. When Hodge noticed him, she came right to him.

"You." He nodded, waving his hand over the food he'd brought to her. "Don't you dare try and butter me up. She just told me that your house is a mansion. And that I didn't have to work anymore."

Raven slipped out and left him there to deal with her "help." He didn't think that was the only reason the two of them had been arguing, but that had been part of it. Gunner asked her to have a seat.

"I got you some milk. I drink it too. Yes, we have a very large house with staff. I've not utilized either the house or the staff all that much, but they'll be there for us." He gave her the second carton of milk when she drank down the first one. "The house was simply too cheap for me to turn down. It belonged to Raven's parents. It was redone by having it painted as well as all the carpets taken out. I don't like carpet either. We can have some put back if you want. Do you like grapes?"

"Yes. All fruit. Why isn't Raven living in her parents' home?" He told her she owned her own home and that she was wealthy. "I suppose you are as well. I don't have anything. I have my retirement from the army, but that's all."

"I am. Here, have half of this sandwich. I wasn't sure you'd care for horseradish sauce, so I got them without." She said she didn't like it. "Neither do I. We have a great deal in common, don't you think?"

"What do you mean, you are? You are what? Wealthy?" He nodded as he opened up the bottle of water and set it by her food. "How wealthy? And why are you telling me this?"

"You asked." She nodded as she took a bite of the sandwich. "How wealthy? Well, very, I guess you could say. Even before I was given the house I'm living in for about fifty cents, I had made some good investments and used my sign-up bonuses as more investments came up. You really don't have to work again if you don't want to.

I wouldn't either, but I'm good at what I do, and it pays well. Here, have some of these grapes, or I'll eat them all."

"Raven knows." He said she knew a great deal about everyone. "I get that. She's more than likely having me investigated too. I don't have much of a past. I don't know shit about me either."

The knock at the door had them both looking in that direction. Gunner was armed, but he knew Hodge wasn't. It didn't stop her from reaching for something to protect herself with, but he didn't comment. His dad, mother, and Molly walked in bearing gifts when the door opened.

"You're beautiful." He laughed when Hodge turned red at Molly's comment. "My goodness, you're like model beautiful. Anyway, I'm Molly Bishop. My mom is Raven, the loudmouth you were dealing with earlier. I know you were because the nurses are talking about how you two were evenly matched when it comes to cursing. I'd like to call you Aunt Andi if that's all right."

"Sure, kid. Whatever you want." Hodge looked at him. "Is that what you're going to call me too? It's fine with me."

"All right. Aunt Andi, it is."

She turned red again, and Gunner laughed. He didn't think having a mate like Andi was going to be all that bad. Gunner handed her another carton of milk and laughed when she asked him if it was because they were all cats now. "I never thought about that. I just like the clean taste of milk. The colder, the better."

She said she liked it that way too. Gunner had another thing to put on his list of things about her he was learning. He decided he'd have a special refrigerator put into their house that would be colder than the fridge, just for milk. Yes, this mate business was just fine with him.

Before You Go...

HELP AN AUTHOR

write a review

THANK YOU!

Share your voice and help guide other readers to these wonderful books. Even if it's only a line or two, your reviews help readers discover the author's books so they can continue creating stories that you'll love. Log in to your favorite retailer and leave a review. Thank you.

AWARD WINNING, BESTSELLING AUTHOR

Kathi Barton, a winner of the Pinnacle Book Achievement award as well as a best-selling author on Amazon and All Romance books, lives in Nashport, Ohio, with her husband, Paul. When not creating new worlds and romance, Kathi and her husband enjoy camping and going to auctions. She can also be seen at county fairs with her husband, who is an artist and potter.

Her muse, a cross between Jimmy Stewart and Hugh Jackman, brings her stories to life for her readers in a way that has them coming back time and again for more. Her favorite genre is paranormal romance, with a great deal of spice. You can visit Kathi on line and drop her an email if you'd like. She loves hearing from her fans. aaronskiss@gmail.com.

Follow Kathi on her blog: http://kathisbartonauthor.blogspot.com/